The Strangest, Craziest People

Chimney Sweep Press Published June 2017.

Printed in the United States of America. First printing 2017.

Library of Congress Preassigned Control Number 2017905097

ISBN 978-0692852996

The Strangest, Craziest People

By Anita Dennis

A Chimney Sweep Press Book

For Jerry and Maddie and the gang

"We are all worms, but I do believe that I am a glow-worm."

—*Winston Churchill*

"A little song, a little dance, a little seltzer down your pants."

—*Chuckles the Clown, "The Mary Tyler Moore Show"*

Prologue

A young girl walks through the dingy basement of a nightclub in Driftwood, New Jersey. The linoleum beneath her feet is curling. She is looking for her father. He is a professional magician, a man whose life is steeped in illusion, and the show is about to start. The humid, too-bright basement smells of makeup, beer and mice. The space consists of a large open area that leads to a narrow, cramped hallway, with low ceilings and doorways to three or four small rooms. There is also a storeroom, with giant containers of pickles, mayo and ketchup, and kegs of beer. Above her, she can hear the sounds of the club's busy main lounge—the lurch and wheeze of band music, the roar of conversation, rattling laughter, off-key singing along with the music. The floor groans as waiters' feet pound from table to table. She knows the rhythm and routine of every night at the club, and she can tell by the songs the band is playing now that the dance music will end soon so that the performers can go on.

She comes to a shabby wooden door marked "Practice Room" and opens it. In the middle of the room stand her father and a woman embracing, their mouths locked together and their arms holding each other tight. Strangely, the first thing the girl notices is the difference in their heights. Her father is a tall man and the woman is tiny. She is young, soft and blond, encased in a pink and gold dress from which her body is fighting to break free. The dress is girlish and unsophisticated, much like a junior prom dress, making the image that much more bewildering. The girl's father is leaning far over to meet the woman's mouth and she is stretching up to meet his, her arms around his neck as if to help her stretch farther. Her back is arched in a way that's both vaguely sexual and comical. She is on tiptoes. When the door opens, the couple freezes, and then the woman, still in a lip lock, makes a slight sputtering noise, like a small animal. As if in a dream, the girl stares at the couple in astonishment. Her immediate thought isn't outrage, disgust or embarrassment, but instead simple puzzlement over why her father would be kissing some chubby little blond.

Loud shouting down the hall behind her breaks the spell. "Ginger? Ted? Where the heck are you?"

The girl, Ginger, slams the practice room door and scurries backwards to head off her mother.

Her mother is barreling along the hallway, nearing the practice room. As usual, she looks annoyed. "Ginger, I can't find your father anywhere. He goes on in 20 minutes." Her mother sighs heavily. Also a performer, she is dark and exotic looking, with heavily made-up eyes that make her look like a haggard Egyptian goddess. She is wrapped in a zebra print dressing gown, and in the harsh light Ginger can see that it is dingy and fraying around the cuffs. Underneath, Ginger knows her mother has on the costume she will wear in her own performance tonight, a gold lamé dress. Ginger loves the shimmer of the material, but now the hem peeking out beneath the robe looks dull and grey in the basement's glare. Her mother's makeup, so striking on the stage, only seems to underline the puffiness of her face in the unyielding shine of the fluorescent panels above her. Unlike the woman that Ginger's father was kissing, who was smooth and puffy, her mother is a scrappy woman with muscular arms. She is also petite, only around five feet tall, but she has long, athletic legs.

Her mother passes a hand across her forehead and closes her eyes. "Gee, I'm tired," she says. "I don't think my health is so good. I get these headaches and these… flashes… sometimes, out of nowhere. Geez, my whole chest is seizing up like a prune."

Behind them there is the sound of a loud thud in the practice room, followed by desperate whispering.

Ginger's mother frowns at the noise. She seems to be considering entering the practice room to investigate.

"I have no idea where Dad is," the girl practically shouts before her mother can become too curious. "He's definitely not in the practice room. No! Not in there! Don't bother looking there. Nope! Nope! Nope! And... I know! I think I got my period!"

The mother sighs again. "So what do you want? Kotex? A tampon? Let's go. I'm short of breath and I still have to find your dumb twit father. Without me, he wouldn't know what to do."

They both head down the hall, away from the couple in the practice room.

That happened in 1973, when I was 15. It was the summer I found out my father was having an affair. But in the end, that was the least of my worries.

Chapter 1

I was raised in a traveling circus. I know, all kids kind of think that, but in my case it was almost true. I really grew up as the unwitting victim of a small band of variety acts, people whose jobs were so weird that they don't exist anymore. My mother was a novelty instrumentalist. Novelty instrumentalists are people who do things with musical instruments that no one else has ever thought of doing before. My mother played the xylophone. You remember, that's the instrument they use to illustrate the letter x in the alphabet when you're in kindergarten. It's a long, flat bed with keys of different sizes. You take two mallets and strike the keys to get a different note from each one. She had been playing since childhood, she told me. She had learned back in the Midwest, a part of the United States that is so dark and scary that she apparently had to get away in a hurry. She ran away to New York as a very young woman, yearning to breathe free. That was where I was born and raised. I was taught to believe New York was the end of the rainbow. But I always wondered, what's it like in those quiet places?

In her act, my mother's specialty was the song "Glowworm." It was such an old song that even in 1973 pretty much nobody remembered it. It was about a worm. That glowed.

So what my mother would do is take a felt worm that was built a bit like a Slinky—and with a big smiling face on it—and string it between her xylophone mallets. It was supposed to look as if the worm was dancing over the xylophone as she played. But that's not the half of it. She had a blacklight on her xylophone that made things glow in the dark. About two-thirds of the way through they would turn off all the house lights and the glow-in-the-dark worm would dance over the xylophone as she played "Glowworm." The undulating worm was all you would see in the darkened room.

My father performed comedy magic. He was also from the Midwest, but he would joke that he was accidentally born in Cleveland and had to find his way back home to Manhattan. He would get people up on stage to participate in rigged tricks with him and hilarity would ensue. He would ask someone to take a card and the whole deck of cards would explode in the air, or he would pull a rabbit out of some guy's pants. Tricks like that. Sometimes he would make balloon animals—squeaky, staticky orange poodles or green giraffes that stuck to your clothes and would not come off—and give them out to the audience as a finale. In 1973, people loved it. Or I guess we traveled a lot, so we found the ones who did love it.

Here's another thing I was raised to understand: New Yorkers were interesting, in some cases simply by virtue of living here, and better than anyone else. We were people who saw celebrities on a street corner or just standing next to you on the subway and pretended not to notice; we were entertained by a 12-year-old playing Bach on the violin for money while standing in a passage in a subway station; we commuted in elevators; we said good night to the neighborhood hookers on the street corner after picking up a paper at the newsstand in the evening. Sometimes we didn't even notice any of that stuff because we were in too big a hurry to be bothered. People in the rest of America got in cars and drove to boring places; that was it, in the gospel according to my family. Kids there sat around waiting to get driven somewhere, imprisoned in a world made up of their house and their yard. That's how my family saw the world. But as long as everyone out there liked balloon acts and xylophones, we were good.

Kids are very observant, especially when it comes to things that set them apart from everyone else in the known universe. My parents' jobs, and struggling to explain them to the other kids in second grade and their nosey parents, made me understand that we lived in a world all our own.

As high-quality show people, we stayed at only the finest hotels when we went on the road, which was often. We were able to do that because my parents, following in a long, beloved show business tradition, had figured out ways to avoid paying the bill. The best strategy was to layer on 12 sets of clothes—everything we owned, basically—leaving behind nothing except the cheap bags we'd brought our clothing in, then walk out. (We kept my mother's xylophone, my father's props and other heavy stuff in lockers that you could rent at every town's bus station.)

Once in a Hilton in Rochester, the hotel clerk asked five-year-old me where we were going, and I'd proudly answered, "We're skipping out of town!" I remember the lobby of that place so well, because it smelled like food that had been left in the refrigerator too long. The clerk kept trying to decide if he should smile, his face twitching uncertainly in the lobby's stark lights. Even as a young child, I always felt a little sorry for those outlanders in those small cities and towns, exiled from New York and doomed to play by the rules. I kind of identified with them in a way, because a lot of the time, in the swirling uncertainty of my parents' world, playing by the rules didn't seem like such a terrible idea to me.

That time in Rochester we did have to pay the bill. The next time they prepped me over and over. "We're going to the zoo! We're going to the zoo!" So there we were in Baltimore, waddling out of the lobby, when the clerk asks, "Where are you going this fine morning?" For a long minute we said nothing, just stared at him as if he had threatened to kill us. Then we all yelled, "Zoo!" and rushed out the door. My father kept a list of hotels to which we could never return.

I found this bewildering when I was very little and mortifying as I got older. I considered refusing to travel with them, but it was too quiet alone at home, with nothing but the sounds of the traffic rumbling by outside and the chatter of the late-night movies that I would watch until dawn, too scared to lie there in silence in the dark. You may think it was difficult to feel alone in New York, but wait until it's 3 a.m. and you're 12 and your parents are entertaining at a convention in Buffalo and the very walls themselves have begun to feel creepy and ominous, when the seeming absence of anyone else anywhere gives you an almost overwhelming urge to start screaming, just to cut the silence. I would sometimes stare out the window, willing a car to pull up with my parents, even though I knew they were not due until the following morning.

No, thanks. The few times I stayed home alone overnight or longer, they would come home reeking of the audience's cigarette smoke, exhausted, full of themselves and probably in need of a bath after a long car or train ride. I would have thrown myself into their arms if I had been that kind of 12-year-old. I decided to stick with them wherever they went after that, like a small animal scrambling to keep up with the rest of the pack.

In addition to staying at posh hotels, we also ate in only the finest restaurants. In New York, there was a restaurant called the Russian Tea Room. It was started by aristocrats—grand dukes and duchesses— who got tossed out of Russia when the country went Communist, way back in the early 1900s. Or at least that's how the legend went. They served heavy, rich, delicious Russian foods and the waiters, who all at least pretended to be Russian, smirked and told dry jokes. "Eat up, dumpling, you must get fat!", a waiter would exclaim as he ladled chicken soup, complete with meat still on the bone, into my bowl. This was funny because no one came to the Russian Tea Room to get fat. In the 1970s, it was a very chic place, full of celebrities and rich nobodies. They liked the Old World charm, but there were limits. Mostly they came for the caviar and blinis—pretty much the chop suey of Russian cuisine—but I was young enough that I loved the soup with who-knew-what floating in it, or the chicken Kiev that squirted butter when the waiter carefully cut into it, something that seemed a little dangerous but was always just a bit of controlled drama in the waiter's skilled hands.

There were beautiful paintings on the walls, the kind an aristocrat might have owned in the sort of beautiful Russian estate that was, by 1973, certainly being used for tractor exhibitions, because the

Communists didn't really go in for glamour. The restaurant was always crowded, the tables were wedged close together, making it very chummy, and everyone seemed excited to be there. And people were a little more relaxed about being rich in those days—it wasn't so much of a spectator sport—so there was a sense of real fun about the place. You always felt as if you were in a world that had disappeared except for this tiny protected spot. As if a loving and fabulously wealthy grandmother had finally found you and brought you home. (This was actually a significant theme of my childhood fantasies—the kind and sane grandmother who would come and rescue me.) Legend has it that Madonna was the coat check girl at the Russian Tea Room for a while, long before she became famous, and if she was she would have been just another lovable eccentric. But it was still a fancy place, so chic it could afford to be a little goofy. Everyone who went there was dressed up, joyously so. This was true in all fancy restaurants in those days. My parents' generation had moved to New York specifically to dress up. They had come to New York to escape the eternal casual Friday that lurked west of the Hudson for as far as the eye could see.

At the Russian Tea Room and any other posh restaurant, here's what my mother would say to the waiter when the check came: "Son, we're friends with Augie, the owner. He told us to come by whenever we wanted, on the house. You tell him the Harrises are here." That was my mother's first shot every time, her initial attempt to get out of paying. We know the owner.

But they were just a little smarter than that at the Russian Tea Room. The maître d' would then come over, look at her coolly and say, "Madam, the owner is not named Augie. There is no Augie here."

My mother would bat her eyes at him, the long fake lashes covered in the kind of green mascara that was sickening even in the 1970s. "No Augie!" She'd turn to my father, bereft. "Ted, this is…."

"It's simply unbelievable," he would exclaim, delivering his line in their prepared script perfectly, his voice tripping higher up the syllables of the word un-be-LIEV-a-ble until it almost squeaked. "My boy, you're saying the owner isn't Augie, er, whatsit? We've known him

9

so long I don't even know his last name." My father had a cultured, sort of English accent, even though he came from Ohio. Although so much about him was inauthentic, he had a certain natural charm that made you give him the benefit of the doubt. He was a tall, lean man, with a good head of dark hair, a long aristocratic nose and eyes that looked tragic and rueful even in his happiest moments. He seemed like a man who was born to sit by a fire in a silk robe, staring into the middle distance with an unread volume of Proust in his lap. None of this pretense put people off, however, because he seemed so vague and disoriented that they wanted to indulge his fantasies.

"Romanov," my mother would toss in helpfully, giving the family name of the tsar who had been killed when the Communists threw out all the aristocrats in Russia. Seven years older than my father, she was tiny, talkative and ready for any fight. My mother had actually been his mentor. They met when she was playing piano and occasional xylophone in a hotel cocktail lounge and he was a waiter hoping to get into show business. Her roommate's boyfriend taught him comedy magic and his career was born.

At the Russian Tea Room, Dad picked up the thread once again. "Right, Augie Romanov," he said. "You don't know Augie Romanov?"

"No, sir. No Augie Romanov."

My parents would exchange shocked glances as I stared at my plate and wished the Communists would come in that minute and kill us all.

"My word, what will we do?" My father would ask.

At this point, the people at the tables near us would have gotten quiet. They wouldn't be staring, because people in New York are way too cool for that sort of thing, but their little ears would be tuned in to our unfolding drama and they would be eyeing each other, secretly delighted at this sad scandal being served up with the borscht. Happily reassuring themselves that they could come to the Russian Tea Room and pay the bill, too.

Then, to make this embarrassing situation completely excruciating, my father would say to my mother in a loud whisper, "I didn't bring any cash, did you?"

"No! I... well, what about a check?

"Yes, that's it. A check!"

"We'll give you a check." My mother would raise her face to the maître d' triumphantly, her large and slightly-too-prominent eyes flashing.

He would smile at her with exquisite regret and say, "I'm afraid we can't take a check."

"My word," Dad would say, drawing out the syllables in his plummy fake British accent.

"Can't take a check," Mom would say. "But—"

The maître d' would lean in close and say quietly, "Mrs. Harris, I'm afraid the check you gave us last time was no good."

Utter silence. And then from my father, "My word."

At this point my mother would start to become indignant. "Son, what is your name?" she'd ask the maître d'.

"Sacha," he'd say. A terribly Russian name that was probably as phony as the check my mother wanted to give him. But I was on his side all the same.

"Sacha. Well, I'm sorry to tell you that you are scaring my daughter."

That was my role in this scam—the Innocent Young Girl Who Should Not Be Put Through This Sort of Thing. My parents used to love a place called Luchow's, down on 14th street, a kind of German beer hall with tuba and accordion players and sausages of all kinds. I don't know why. They usually had pretty sophisticated tastes, but maybe it was the surreal nature of the place that appealed to them.

Anyway, to prevent us from being arrested the last—and I should say final—time we went to Luchow's, I had been forced to cry pretty hard. Accompanied by some shrieking, even, because my mother kept pinching me. Otherwise I'm pretty sure the police would have been called. We had used up a lot of goodwill at Luchow's, it seems.

Back at the Russian Tea Room, I could feel them all looking at me, but I would try to ignore them and pretend I was in a better place. So my mother would say it again, in a louder and angrier voice. "Sacha, I'm afraid I'm going to have to ask you to stop scaring my daughter, GINGER." She would growl my name in a husky and very scary whisper.

Unable to avoid my part in this scam any longer, I would snap my head up and recite, "What's happening to us, Mommy? Are they going to put you and Daddy in jail?"

"You can see she's becoming hysterical," Mom would say. They would all look at me, but I had gone back to pretending to be in a coma. My mother would elbow me sharply in the ribs and I would relent.

"Please help us, sir," I would finally say to the maître d'. It was not part of the script, but it was sincere.

He would say, so softly that you could barely hear, "All right. We'll take a check, Mrs. Harris."

Once he was gone, my parents could hardly keep the delighted smiles off their faces.

"We were good," my mother purred.

"We were bloody good," my father agreed.

"Shut up," I said, still staring at my plate.

"This girl is a pro," my father said, smiling indulgently at me.

"Shut up," I said.

"No matter what hacks we are," he said, "we've produced a lot of talent."

"We are not hacks—" my mother began.

"Shut up or I'm not going to restaurants with you two anymore."

I was embarrassed by them, that goes without saying. But I also felt an icicle of panic at these times. I had seen them haggling regularly with the manager of our apartment-hotel, my mother gesticulating indignantly and pointing at me, parked on a chair in the lobby, the innocent victim. I assumed that she was negotiating with him because we didn't pay the rent on time. Also, based on the long dry periods between some of their shows, I had to wonder sometimes if a few of the items in the fridge were shoplifted. When my dad brought home a steak or my mother triumphantly waved a bag of shrimp in our faces, all I could think of was how close they must have come to being arrested, how terrifying it would be to see them dragged away in handcuffs, because I couldn't believe they'd been able to pay for such expensive items. I knew that my parents saw this as a game, but I wondered, what would happen if they kicked us out of our apartment? If we ran out of food? If the cops walked in right now and took them away, amid the borscht and samovars? I didn't think that a kindly couple at the Russian Tea Room would rush over to adopt me, setting me up in a pastel-hued bedroom in their spacious Westchester home. With a breakfast nook and a big yard. No, I didn't think that would happen. I thought that everyone in the restaurant would most likely look away, going back to their blinis and politely ignoring the girl who was left behind.

After trouble at a restaurant, we would wait a while until this Sacha had been replaced by another Sacha, then go back and try it again. You don't have to live like poor people just because you don't have money. That was a family value in our house. "We can't afford everything we deserve and we don't want to die deserving, right?" my mother would say, practically singing the words like a hymn. And if you were going to cheat someone out of dinner, you might as well cheat them out of the best dinner in town. Ducking out of diners was for con-artist wannabes. My parents were pros.

I was glad I didn't really know any other kids, because I definitely had the most embarrassing parents. But I will say that once you've been thrown out of enough fancy restaurants and hotels, then posh people and posh places don't scare you anymore. You can sail into any situation as if you belonged there, because what's the worst that can happen? If they throw you out, well, you know that routine. There is a certain confidence in knowing you are inured to embarrassment. I have watched many domineering loudmouths turn into mumbling, obsequious ninnies once they got through the doorway of a five-star restaurant, and thought, "Come on, it's just people with money." So my childhood was not entirely wasted.

Our own eccentric lifestyle was not the only quirk in my childhood. My parents' friends were as close to circus acts as you could come without actually smelling the popcorn. One woman was a glass player. I mean it, a glass player. She would line up about a dozen glasses, each one filled with a different amount of water. Then she would wet her finger and rub it around the rim of the glass, creating a sound. Each glass made a different tone, or note, depending on how much water was in it. She could play "My Country, 'tis of Thee," "Oh Susanna," "Row, Row, Row Your Boat." Anything you wanted to hear. She had cottony, softly waved blond hair and a permanent smile on her face. Which came first: the endless optimism or the need to keep going despite the many challenges that must come when you make music using tableware? Where had she learned this stuff? Was she also from the Midwest, and this is what it did to you? Maybe it was a family tradition, or was she a prodigy or a changeling whose unique talent for playing glasses was discovered during her girlhood? So many mysteries to consider.

Then there was Sally Snively and Her Eyelash Review. That was the name of the act. Sally was a little firecracker of a woman from Dallas who had actually married a rich Texas oilman and was using her fortune to break herself into show business. She had hired about five tall showgirls, who would parade around handing out fake eyelashes to the women in the audience while she sang. They eventually went back to Texas, tired of the city or chasing some new oil deal, I guess.

In the meantime, she was kind and funny and for the year or so that she was around I was the only kid in fourth grade with false eyelashes.

You had to give them some credit, this ragtag band of show people. Although they may not have been particularly attractive or talented, even, my parents and their friends were in their own ways larger than life, in most part because of their completely delusional self-confidence. It gave them a light in their eyes, a certain presence when they entered the room that did set them apart from other people. Their problem was that they fit in only in a world that was quickly vanishing, and may have only ever existed in their own minds.

Let me explain. Once upon a time, there was something called vaudeville. This was before television and even before movies. There were theatres, but instead of showing movies they had shows with one crazy act after another. Acrobats, animal acts, singing groups, xylophone players—they had them all. About 100 years ago, my parents would have fit right in.

Then movies were invented and many theatres started showing them instead of having shows. Playing a movie was a lot cheaper than paying all those acts—and having an orchestra to play for them—so it made sense. Then TV came along, and people didn't even need to bother leaving their houses to be entertained. Fewer and fewer theatres featured live performances by people like my parents. First theatres in the big cities stopped having them, then the smaller cities, then the really small cities, then virtually no one at all booked acts like my parents. That was how things stood in 1973.

Later, when I grew up, people asked me why I didn't go into show business myself. I would say, "Too much smiling." Because these people, these very, very committed people who would twist themselves into pretzel shapes if they could make an act out of it, boy, they smiled all the time. Like their lives depended on it. And given what was about to happen, I think maybe they did.

*

15

The Upper West Side of Manhattan, where we lived, at the time was a glorious wreck. Much like many of the people who lived there, it was shabby and sketchy and very unfashionable but still glamorous. There is a musical called "Brigadoon" in which a magical Scottish village appears out of the mist only one day every hundred years. That's how I think of the Upper West Side of the time, as a place that has vanished and that I keep thinking may one day reappear, if only the rich people from out of town would go home. Small apartment buildings were crammed with struggling young people who were delighted to be living in a dingy flat with unreliable heat and plumbing. On the side streets, there were brownstones full of librarians, taxi drivers, bookkeepers, secretaries, the people who kept the city working all day, mixed in with aspiring writers and actors willing to live in close quarters for a while in hopes of future success, all looking for a room to come home to. The buildings lining the avenues were like castles, taking up half a block and dotted with elaborate carvings, or square and solid and splendid. Along their first floors there was the occasional supermarket, but mostly small shops or restaurants. I would like to tell you that the shop owners were all friendly and knew your name, but you know I'd be kidding, right? Because New York used to be the place where people came if they couldn't get along with anyone in their hometowns, then you put all those people together and watched what happened.

The smells: the aroma of the bakeries selling babka and macaroons, the earthy scent of boot polish from a shoemaker's shop, the briny odor of ice melting onto the street from a fish store, the smoky, tarry odor on summer nights that we referred to as "New Jersey." The smell—and steamy warmth—of something being boiled beyond recognition that came wafting through the building when you arrived home at twilight on a November evening. And the colors: the florid hues of former showgirls, now in their 70s. They gathered on the benches on the islands in between the lanes on Broadway every day dressed like fidgety tropical birds, in bright-colored clothing and full theatre makeup, trading gossip while hacking away from their two-pack-a-day smoking habits. The bright white of the scarf fluttering behind the opera singer sweeping up Broadway, his head filled with the notes of a new aria. The blacks and autumn colors of theatre actors, maybe a little past their prime, strolling home from dinner at the local Chinese restaurant, trading theatre gossip and hilarious tales of backstage fiascos. The grey and white flicker of the papers at the newsstands on virtually every other corner, brimming with stories. The sounds you heard were mainly the white noise of traffic, of a truck rumbling a manhole as it passed or an ancient taxi clattering down the avenue. At night, there was the constant hum of cars flying down the West Side Highway, and it was comforting to hear them out there, reassurance that someone was keeping the world running while I slept.

We lived in a blocky apartment-hotel in the West 90s, a place where you weren't obligated to sign a long-term lease. It was a place whose glory days were behind it, an outpost for people of modest means who were between commitments. The lobby was usually full of people, as if there was a party going on. The sagging couches were all snagged by old ladies, not the former show girls, but savvy birds who watched the neighborhood and analyzed the comings and goings. Like most places, it was choked with a fog of cigarette smoke.

New York was known at the time as a dangerous place where you wouldn't want to raise kids, but I think that was an ingenious PR campaign to keep the tourists out. With all the many sharp-eyed and sharp-elbowed old ladies, bossy store owners and indignant mothers watching out for their kids, there were many people ready to stick their noses into your business if you needed help. I rarely felt afraid at night. With a curious nature and parents who were distracted much of the time, I can tell you that it was often hard to get a seat on the subway after midnight amid the bustle of people heading to their next important destination. I would be swept along in a crowd who would have been eager—delighted actually—to beat up anyone who might have posed a danger to me.

I loved these solo nighttime rambles, being part of the surging, excited crowd and yet a free agent in the ongoing party and spectacle of Manhattan at night. I loved the quiet moments, too. The middle-aged Hispanic doorman sweeping in front of an apartment building at 1 a.m., who murmured "God bless you, dear," as I passed. The elderly couple, both wearing hats on a summer evening, long after wearing hats all the time had gone out of style, who stopped and chastely kissed each other on the lips as they waited for a light to change on Broadway. Or the band of noisy, dressed-up Southerners, sitting on a bench in the middle of Times Square at 2 a.m. on one New Year's Day, after the party was over and everyone else had gone home. One of them, a big blond with large liquid brown eyes, leaned over as I passed them, stretching out a long arm toward me. "Hey, honey, do you want a hat?" She held one of those metallically shiny cardboard top hats that people used to wear on New Year's Eve. And I took it, because even though New Year's for me usually meant watching melancholy adults get tipsy, she was inviting me to share in her party, her joy, and that was nice.

Coming home on the subway at night—all of us passengers together in a light-filled tube hurtling through the darkness—sometimes I would imagine what I would do if I just kept going past my stop, heading for who knows what adventures. But before I got too far with my fantasies I would find myself wondering who would come looking for me, or if anyone would. I was a part of my parents' tribe—I could outline the group's every custom and belief—but I was not really one of them. I took no joy in performance, whether on stage or in daily life, or in outsmarting the system or living on the edge. Outsmarting the system, my god, I would have been delighted with a system of any kind in our unpredictable lives; where could I sign up? So, with quietly suffocating anxiety, I would sit on the train and wonder if they would notice my absence if I took off, or if I would just end up rattling back and forth between Van Cortlandt Park in the Bronx and South Ferry in Manhattan—the two ends of the Broadway local—forever. With those fears chasing me, I would elbow my way toward the subway door at my stop and race home in the still evening air.

Then I would go to bed, listening to my parents and their friends in the living room, playing cards and telling stories.

"Marty, tell them about the time that the pigs got loose during the blind violin player's act. Tell them, Marty!"

Chapter 2

When I was small, I would often accompany my mother when she went on errands around our neighborhood and around Midtown Manhattan. I never liked the beauty salon, which smelled of nail polish remover and hair dye and was overheated by the hair dryers that women were still sitting under at that time. This was before women brought their children to salons to get mani/pedis, so I was relegated to the waiting area, where I read magazines that featured bizarre new hairdos or talked about starlets' love lives. As I got older, I continued to follow her around out of a kind of routine. One day that summer when I was 15, we had two stops to make before heading to lunch with an old friend of the family.

The day had already started out weird. My parents were both out in the morning. My father had been away for a couple of days at a show in Pennsylvania and my mother was getting groceries. I was lying on the floor watching "The Prisoner of Zenda" on TV when there was a knock at the door. I opened it to find a small, pretty woman with dark hair. She had a strong jaw that reminded me of my mother's, and twinkly blue eyes. She was wearing a silky soft pink dress that I could tell was expensive and carrying a beige ostrich purse.

We both stared at each other for a while. Finally, I raised an eyebrow, indicating an interest in what she wanted, to break the standoff. She nodded, as if she got that she was supposed to talk but was still collecting her thoughts.

"Are you... the maid?" she asked.

I snorted. "I'm the daughter," I said.

She shook her head as if startled, then made a face that seemed to be a mixture of horror and pity. "Ginger," she said, not to me, but calling up the name from some deep recess of her mind. "You're Ginger."

"Who are you?"

"Is Dor—. Is your mother home?"

"Not right now. Can I help you?" I had spent a lot of time playing the obnoxious assistant dealing with people who called or stopped by when my parents weren't around and I really enjoyed it. They were sometimes people that my parents owed money to, and I had learned the value of starting off by being offensive and negotiating down from there.

"Look," she said. She reached into her purse, her precise movements giving off a wave of flowery perfume. Her fingernails were covered in a nice shade of pink polish, but they were a little spotty around the edges, so I could tell she had done them herself. Given the quality of her clothes and purse, I decided she was someone who wanted to buy good things but didn't want to waste money on something she could do herself, like a manicure. I liked her a little for that.

She wrote something on a small pad with a little gold pen. I was speculating on whether it was real gold when she shoved a tiny piece of paper in my face. "Dorothy, Please call Lorraine," it said, followed by a phone number.

"Can you please give this to your mother, dear?"

"I don't know who you are."

"It's all right. Your mother will know."

22

"What are you, from the police?" I said, reveling in my obnoxiousness. I wanted to shock her, but again that look of horror and pity came over her.

"Oh, no, dear. It's nothing like that." She stood staring at me for a moment, then squeezed my hand briefly before walking quickly down the hall toward the elevator.

"A strange woman came when you were gone," I told my mother when she got back.

"What strange woman?" When I handed her the note, she shook her head, then snorted. "She was here, this woman?" She shook her head again. She crumpled the note up in her hand, but I noticed that she threw it into her purse, and not into the garbage.

Our first errand that day took us to Lord & Taylor, a posh department store where my mother worked part time sometimes because, as she explained, even the top stars needed to make a little money on the side. She worked there pretty steadily during the Christmas rush, but she also picked up days throughout the year. That day we were going to pick up her check for the last couple of weeks of work.

There was a special entrance for employees. It was on a grimy and not at all glamorous side street in the high 30s, but I loved that street because it was filled with garment center storefronts. One sold buttons, with walls full of all shapes and sizes and colors and styles. There were ones made of wood or horn, ones shaped like ship anchors and ones with elaborate carvings. You could go in there, as I did sometimes when I wanted a change from waiting for my mother in the employee cafeteria, and you could imagine all the many outfits that would have those buttons, and the people who would wear them. There was another store that was just hats and feather boas. The people who owned the place, Mr. and Mrs. Bagheri, would let you try on anything. In sixth grade, thanks to their generosity, I wore a different color feather boa just about every day. Another favorite was a store that sold only rhinestone jewelry, great sparkling piles of it. My mother and her friends often went there to pick up pieces for their stage wardrobes. They strode around, trying on jewelry and glittering like the princesses of West 38th Street.

Inside Lord & Taylor, I sat on a bench outside the personnel office while my mother went in to get her check. Even the employee corridors, which were dark and utilitarian, had a respectful hush, as if talking too loudly would somehow bother the customers, who were picking out expensive outfits on the other side of the wall. There was a woman named Beverly, a tall blond who had once been a store model, who was in charge of part timers. She and my mother got along well, so they often chatted a while. As I sat there, two saleswomen came out. One was a slim blond with big eyes, just a bit too big, and another had a mass of wavy black hair and a curvy figure.

"There's Dorothy Harris," the dark-haired one muttered, looking back into the personnel office. "I always feel bad about her."

"Why?" the blond asked.

Her friend stopped, just a few feet from where I was sitting. I loved to eavesdrop, so I pulled the *Daily News* up in front of my face so they would assume I wasn't paying attention.

"I had a thing with her husband," the dark one whispered.

The blond barked a sharp laugh. "Everyone's had a thing with her husband, Janie."

I was always surprised when my mother was right. My mother had taught me that people in fashion retail were vipers. In her description, they had sharp teeth and sharp claws, which would not be zoologically correct for a snake, but it did paint a picture. "I like them," she told me. "They're like my friends. But they are vicious, and don't forget it." And here were these women, each maybe 10 or 15 years younger than my parents, claiming to have fooled around with my dad. I wouldn't have said my parents were a wildly happy couple. A lot of their conversations were actually arguments, but I was sure that day that it hadn't come to that.

Our next stop was at the office of my parents' agent, a man named Izzy Zimmerman. Izzy's office was in a small building on a side street between Broadway and 7th Avenue in Midtown. The lobby was a color people might think of as faux marble, kind of dullish white with a lot of shadowy sections that I think might have actually been stains. It was always dank, with a sour smell that I had decided must be the scent of old cigars marinating in a tub of water somewhere in the building. I don't know why I thought that. When you're a kid, though, a lot of what goes on or what you experience makes no sense. You sometimes have to struggle to come up with explanations for the world adults have built, so you end up getting creative.

There wasn't a doorman or a guard, but there was always a bunch of guys in workmen's uniforms lingering around a desk in the lobby. They were always friendly and eager to say hello, in a way that made them seem guilty about something. You started out liking them and then you thought, wait, what are they up to? Straight ahead, past the elevator, was a door that was always propped open by a single chipped and scratched wooden chair with a maroon fake leather seat. Inside the doorway, it was dark and dirty, and there was some kind of equipment in there: boilers or used air conditioners or industrial floor polishers—I'm not sure what exactly. In my experience, this describes the lobbies of 90% of the small office buildings in Midtown Manhattan.

Izzy's office was on the fourth floor. The elevator was small—four people might have been a bit cramped—and old. The walls were made of shiny metal panels in what must have once seemed like a modern, jet-set finish. Now at least one of the panels was always loose, and it rattled so much during the ride that you almost didn't notice the alarming squealing noise that the elevator machinery made as it worked desperately to drag you up to the fourth floor. The light behind one of the buttons you had to push for your floor was always out. Again, this generally describes most of the elevators in small Midtown office buildings that I have known.

The door to Izzy's office was half wood and half frosted glass. The name of his agency—Zimmerman Productions—was marked on the glass in gold letters. There was no receptionist. You just walked right in and there was Izzy, a big man with a mane of white hair and intelligent eyes.

"Dorothy!" he said, somewhat uneasily. "And your lovely daughter Pepper!"

"My name is Gin-" I started to say before my mother cut me off.

"What have you got for us, Izzy?" she said, easing herself into a seat before him without an invitation.

"Well, of course, you have the summer at Curly's—"

"Yes, that's a given, we get that every year. What else have you got? I hope you're not going to disappoint me again." She leaned toward him, confidential and menacing. "I've had expressions of interest from Richie Bright," my mother said, mentioning the name of another agent, as we sat down.

Izzy put his large hands on the desk in front of him and sighed. Everyone still wore business dress to work in those days, but many men wore short-sleeved dress shirts when it got a little warmer. Izzy didn't. He was wearing a blue dress shirt with white pinstripes, with the sleeves rolled up just a little to show hefty wrists. He had a gold tie pin that was a quarter note and a large gold watch. There were foot-high stacks of paper on his desk and a small air conditioner droned uselessly in the window behind him, but he still looked elegant, somehow, in his pinstripe shirt. As if he had read my complimentary thoughts, he reached into a bowl and handed me a peppermint candy. "Here you go, Sagebrush," he said.

"Now, Dorothy. I got three weekends in the Catskills for Ted when you come back. I also have a wedding for you at a synagogue in Hicksville on September 23rd. For the moment, that's all I got." He looked up at her, his face and shoulders set. "Of course, I could get you cruises. On a cruise, they would like the balloons and the xylophone. Love it, maybe."

My mother sat back in her chair. "You're insulting me," she said.

"Insulting? Never. You're great acts, it's just a little slow now. You go to Curly's. It'll pick up in the fall."

He was standing now, ushering us out. He was smiling, but I knew he was waiting for my mother's well-known temper to blow. The office was so small that we had to walk backwards to get past our chairs and out the door. And then we were in the hall.

"So long, Dorothy," he said, closing the door. "Pleasure to see you, Cinnamon."

My mother stood in the hall, staring at his door and vibrating. All up and down the corridor, there were small offices with small businesses like Izzy's. Other theatrical agents, printers, photographers, a dentist, even a detective agency and one place called The Institute of Hair. The dentist's office, I believe, was giving off a minty medicinal smell that permeated the air. Whatever all the people in those offices were doing, it was silent in the hallway. My mother continued to stand there, breathing abnormally deeply, taking in great lungfuls of thick summer air. Then she turned to me, and I remembered a movie about zombies I had accidentally watched one night, because her face was very pale but her eyes seemed to be on fire. I suddenly became aware of the pool of sweat that had formed around the small of my back when we were in Izzy's office.

"Three weekends for Ted in the Catskills," she finally hissed. "Crooooo-ses," she said, drawing out the word for several syllables through sneering lips. She started vibrating again.

"I will not be treated this way," she said, pretty loudly now, grabbing my arms and shaking me. "I cannot be treated this way."

"I know," I said, trying to get my arms loose. I think my father and I both figured out early on how to avoid setting off her temper, but sometimes you just got caught in the crossfire.

"The things I do for these goddamn people," she began, her voice rising with each word until she was basically hollering.

I looked quickly at my watch. "Hey, are we going to be late to see Larry?"

Her gaze, which had been roaming around the corridor crazily, snapped to mine. "Larry," she said, nodding. "Let's go see Larry." Turning to push the button for the elevator, she laughed, stopped abruptly, then laughed again. "Larry, of course. What would Larry think if he saw me like this?" she asked, giggling a little weirdly, like random hiccups. "What would he think? He'd never believe it." She sighed, smiled and slammed her fist hard on the button for the elevator, which was refusing to come. "Let's go see Larry."

Chapter 3

"If you just keep on being great at what you do, Dorothy, I'm going to put the world at your feet."

"Stop, Larry, you're being silly."

"You make me silly, sweetheart."

My mother had someone she considered an admirer, a man named Larry Davenport. Whenever she saw him she brought me along, because, as I'd overheard her tell a friend, he was a little dangerous. Usually we went to the 21 Club for lunch with him. It was considered one of the most exclusive places in the city at the time, housed in an old townhouse in the heart of Midtown on 52nd Street. The entrance was guarded by a row of lawn jockeys and you walked past them down a set of steps to get in.

My parents met Larry before I was born, while they were on the road in Minneapolis, I believe. He was a singer who was just starting out in the business and they had befriended him, allowing him to sleep on a couch in their hotel room when he ran out of cash and hadn't yet realized that paying was optional. He was about a decade younger than my mother. He became successful very quickly, beginning in the small clubs or theatres where my parents worked but moving on to nicer lounges in better and better hotels. Then Larry was booked on TV on "The Ed Sullivan Show," a weekly hour-long festival of acts like my parents, as well as comedians and singers, and on a couple of other similar shows. Once you performed on TV, you were at least a little bit famous, and he had quickly been in demand for shows and clubs around the country that wanted performers who were something like a celebrity.

When he was in New York, though, he always got in touch with my parents and other old friends from his early days. And he indulged in an insistent teasing flirtation with my mother. He was charming, but in a completely different way from my father. My father, with his rumbling ersatz British accent and his lazy elegance, seemed like a different generation from Larry, even though he was only a couple of years older. Larry had softer features and fuller lips, and he was shorter and more muscular. In contrast to my father's reserved courtliness, he would burst into a room and tell jokes that would make the women giggle and the men chortle despite themselves. If my father had decided to be the wry British gentleman, then Larry was the cheerful, energetic American guy.

The people at 21 loved him. "You are the best!" he would shout at the waiter as he brought lunch, burgers for Larry and me and lobster salad for my mother. We sat scrunched together at a small table in the bar room, the prime location. Lauren Bacall was huddled in a corner, wearing dark glasses and allowing a feline smile now and then as she was regaled with stories by an earnest young man. Zsa Zsa Gabor, a bubbly Hungarian who was possibly the first person to be famous for being famous, was holding court a few tables away, gesturing with a multi-colored scarf as she spoke. But even with these bona fide celebrities, there still seemed to be an attentive group of waiters ready for Larry whenever he needed something, since his star was rising and who knew where it would take him.

Over drinks while we waited for our meal, my mother told Larry about her frustration with the kinds of bookings she and my father were getting. Even I had noticed that the audiences were dwindling and that there were more and more weekend nights when we all sat home watching sitcoms. My parents had been arguing about whether she should take on more hours at Lord & Taylor and he should devote more time to his part-time job as a maître d' at a place in Midtown called Chandler's. My mother believed there was a tipping point, when you'd worked so much at your day job that you woke up one morning and noticed that show business had slipped away from you. She seemed firmly committed to preventing that from happening.

"I know my big break is out there, Larry," she said at lunch that day. "I just can't get it in my grasp."

Larry watched her thoughtfully. "I want to make you a proposition, Dorothy," he finally said.

"Larry, my daughter is here. I have to ask you to behave yourself." But there was a slight smile on her lips as she said it.

"No, my dear, this time you misunderstand me!" He winked and leaned toward her, smiling rakishly. I always felt that Larry was just being entertaining when engaged in this light flirting. There was no question he was genuinely fond of my father, and he only teased my mother this way when he wasn't around. "I had something completely different in mind. What are you doing this summer?"

"We're going to that little club on the Jersey shore. We go there every summer. His whole show revolves around us. No chance of losing that. He's going to want us coming back forever."

"Perfect!" Larry rubbed his hands together and somehow managed to lean closer to my mother. "That will give you a chance to polish up your already excellent act, because I have a few things in mind for you."

My mother slowly sucked the liquid off the stirrer from a new Bacardi cocktail that the waiter had just delivered. It was a very sweet, very red drink that had a nice kick of rum. She had a habit of not finishing them, so I usually did it for her. Above us, a couple of hundred toys—airplanes, blimps, racecars—all donated by celebrities who were 21 regulars, hung from the ceiling. Around us the room was a riot of red-and-white checked tablecloths.

"Like what things in mind for me?" she asked, a certain disdainful suspicion in her voice.

But Larry wasn't listening. "Liza!" he called in an excited whisper to a somewhat stunned Liza Minnelli. Not yet 30, she had that year won an Oscar for "Cabaret." She was walking by us and quietly aiming for the door with her head down. She looked up reluctantly at Larry's call, but then clearly recognized him and smiled warmly and nodded, still backing towards the exit.

"Like what," my mother barked at Larry, watching him wave enthusiastically to the retreating star.

"I've got a plan and a backup plan. First, I'll tell you the backup plan, because I think you're going to like it."

"Dazzle me," my mother said. She swayed back and forth in her seat a bit and I tried to remember how many cocktails she'd actually finished.

"Radio City Music Hall." Larry enunciated each word separately. The gorgeous art deco theatre was known as the home of the Rockettes, but the shows there also sometimes included other performers. In fact, one of Larry's many early big breaks involved being the featured tenor in one year's Christmas show. It was several steps above the kind of place my parents usually played, and would certainly be a good locale to be seen by local agents who didn't know my mother or had forgotten her. And you would be amazed at how many weird acts they crammed into those Christmas and Easter shows in those days, so if anyone was going to book a xylophone act, Radio City Music Hall might actually be the place.

I looked to see her reaction. She was staring past Larry and blinking rapidly. I could tell she was excited because she looked sick to her stomach.

"Okay," she finally gasped. "What's the big plan if that's the backup?"

Larry leaned in even farther. "Dorothy, you're a beautiful and talented woman, so we have to aim high. So, I'm thinking, 'The Dean Martin Show.'"

My mother swiveled her head toward Larry and gurgled something semi-verbal. Along with Frank Sinatra, Dean Martin was a member of the Rat Pack, a group of performers who were sort of the epitome of early '60s cool. While Frank Sinatra was the tightly wound neighborhood kid with a soft heart, Dean Martin was the languid, easygoing guy who was looking for a good time. He had a variety TV show where he sang, told nearly naughty jokes and flirted with all the women. There were also performances by guest stars, usually comedians or singers. It was definitely more difficult to picture him fitting a xylophonist into his lineup. Older established stars were somewhat terrified of the relentless and expanding success of rock music, and an entire culture that seemed to be turning against the gracious past. I didn't think a xylophone act would help Dean establish his street cred, or whatever we would have called it at the time.

"Larry," my mother breathed, almost with a warning tone in her voice. She looked terrified.

"I know some people, cutie. I hope you'll let me see what I can do. I'd love to do whatever I can for you. I hate hearing you talk about your disappointment."

"Well, of course," she said, flat out gushing now. "How could I say no?"

"Larry!" A lithe young woman with a blond pixie haircut dropped into his lap and kissed him on the cheek, stretching out her long legs as she leaned back.

"I didn't know you were in town." She wrinkled her nose at him and ran her fingers through his hair. She had enormous brown eyes and a perfect complexion. Although I was 15, even I probably looked about 20 years older than her, she was so fresh and dewy.

"Sammy, my sweet, it's so good to see you! I want you to meet some old and dear friends of mine. This is Dorothy Harris and her daughter Ginger."

My mother raised a steeply arched black eyebrow and smiled. "A pleasure to meet you."

"Are you coming to Stewie's tonight? Say you'll come so we can catch up. You can bring your friends." She turned and twinkled at us, the loveliest thing in the room. "I missed you at Roger's last time. You told me you'd come, bad boy." She blew him a kiss and tripped off to another table.

When Larry had disentangled himself from her, my mother slid her hand toward him. Physical affection was not unusual between them because he was like family, but it was a funny time for her to start holding hands.

"So, what's our next step?"

Larry, who was waving at Sammy as she left, turned his attention back to us. "You three go to the shore, have a good time and I'll be in touch."

"We won't see you all summer," she said, almost pouting. I was ready to barf.

"Don't worry, Duchess," he said. "You'll be hearing from me a lot."

We left 21 and walked up 5th Avenue, arm in arm with Larry in the center. No matter whom we met—from a local gossip columnist to the doorman at the Plaza Hotel—Larry introduced my mother as a talented performer who was going to be on "The Dean Martin Show" soon.

"No, Estelle, it was Joan Crawford in that movie."

"No, you're crazy. It was Betty Grable."

"I think you mean Bette Davis, and it wasn't her anyway."

"If that was Bette Davis then who's Betty Grable?"

"The one with the legs."

As we came into our hotel, two bickering old ladies with large glasses that made them look like giant bugs turned toward us hopefully. Although the lobby was usually bustling, tonight these two sat alone in a cloud of cigarette smoke. The light in our lobby seemed especially harsh and cold as we came home that night. The bickering lobby ladies looked grumpy and faded, and the whole place was missing its usual festive air. The elevator smelled of pickles. At dinner, my mother and I looked at each other across the table, a foldup one that we set up in the middle of the small living room each night. I wondered if she was thinking, as I was, about the stark difference between our cozy hearth and the giddy energy at 21 and in Larry's Midtown haunts. The Upper West Side waltzed, it was true, but the orchestra sounded a little sad and old after we had spent the day listening to the restless jazz of a brighter world.

I could hear the music, too. After years of being the weird girl, I wouldn't have minded being swept up in the lives of the famous, being vindicated for being different. But even if you're chronically cynical you can still tell when something's actually going to go wrong, and that summer it was hard not to notice the danger signs. My parents lived a life in opposition to the normal course of the rest of the world, to the reality I could clearly see and that they didn't seem to notice. When my mother grabbed on to the possibilities Larry offered, she reminded me of a blackjack player whose hand could clearly never win, yet she kept yelling "Hit me again!" And you had to win sometimes, right? I don't think I fully understood at that age that instead of chips, she was in danger of losing the many years that she had invested in the possibility of success, of stardom even. When she was a young woman, she had probably thought, "People will always want entertainment. What could possibly go wrong?" Like a worker on her first day at the rotary-phone factory, she had never imagined that it might all disappear from beneath her feet one day when it seemed much too late to start over.

Chapter 4

When the warm weather came, we got away from the city. In the summer of 1973, my parents were booked for three months at a club called Curly's Sea Shack in Driftwood, New Jersey. This would be the fifth summer they would work there. Driftwood was a beach town, right on the Atlantic Ocean, and during the summer it was filled with vacationing families anxious to watch a woman play the glasses and a man make animal balloons. They could have watched television or movies, but they were on vacation, for goodness sake. Something about going to a club made it all seem more exciting.

Every week a new group of families came for their seven days of holiday by the shore, so Curly could hire one set of acts for the entire summer and get a new audience each Saturday night. Late at night when the show was over, Curly played Beach Boys and Beatles records. The kids in the audience danced and their parents drank heavily. Everyone was happy.

Driftwood had that haunting shore town smell of crumbling wooden piers drenched in years of sea salt. I always relaxed a little when I first smelled it because I loved beach towns. The beach and the boardwalk seemed never ending, so I could walk for miles in happy solitude. Driftwood also smelled of popcorn, which was stored in glass cubes at boardwalk stands, right next to the cotton candy machines.

Every year my parents and their friends talked in worried tones about how it was on the verge of being taken over by kids. In 1973, the whole world was on the verge of being taken over by kids. The

Watergate hearings, which were investigating a scandal that would force President Nixon to resign the following year, began in May, seeming to cap all the unrest of the 1960s. For as long as a decade, people of my parents' generation had been warily sidestepping the angry impatience of people in their teens and twenties. Today, it is young children who have invaded, rolling in a squadron of strollers into the most exclusive stores and restaurants, bringing along their cheerful vocalizing and brightly colored toys. They are everywhere, from the beer-drenched corners of venerable saloons to the tea room at the Plaza. In 1973, it was teenagers, aggressive and acne-scarred, who were overrunning the world.

In Driftwood, there was a tattoo parlor, then an exotic and taboo idea, on a side street on the edge of town. There were two amusement piers, one with rides that played circus music and catered to small kids and another with roller coasters and other more adventurous rides for older ones. That second pier drew a "bad element," my parents and their friends insisted, but all I ever saw there were kids like me.

Perhaps not quite like me, actually. At that time, I dressed in a style that would be considered Goth today, except without the piercings and the tattoos. I had grown my straight brownish hair long and dyed it jet black and almost always wore all black.

This set me apart in school, even though I went to a school intended for kids whose lives were outside the norm. In late elementary school, my parents had somehow managed to get me a scholarship at a private school called the Academy for Talented Children. It was specially designed to accommodate the schedules of kids in show business, who might have to take off five days to be in a commercial or leave early every Wednesday to perform in a Broadway matinee. They were extremely perky, outgoing children who would sometimes stand in the hall and burst into a song about canned ham or laundry detergent, if they had recently been in a commercial for those items. I did not perform myself, I wasn't perky and I never sang about canned ham, but the school was great about dealing with my parents' schedule when they took me on the road with them. And

I did feel I shared something in common with my classmates. We all understood that our families were different from others in ways that were hard to explain to people who weren't familiar with the multifaceted strangenesses of show business. Many of us were also expected to carry on the family tradition.

"She hates school," my mother would tell her friends proudly. "Who needs it? It's full of kids."

My mother did not have her sights set on a conventional career for me. "She's gonna be a great actress, that's what I think," she would say, sitting for hours with other performers over coffee in a luncheonette or in one of the last surviving Automats, a great tradition among out-of-work show people. They would all scrutinize me, searching for signs of greatness.

"God knows, she's so dramatic already," my mother would tell them. "Mostly I see her on the stage, but she could go out to the coast now and then, do some movies, TV, soak up some bucks and come home. Buy me and Ted a nice little place in Florida."

Her friends sighed and nodded appreciatively.

My mother's dreams were in direct contrast to my accomplishments on stage. The first time I had ever auditioned for anything—I believe it was a hot dog commercial—was when I was five. There had been a frenzy of activity to present me at my finest. My parents had scrubbed me until I squeaked, curled my hair and dressed me in something itchy that made a crackling noise when I walked. When we got there, I stood up in front of the casting directors, threw up, curtsied, then walked out. Every couple years they tried again, with much the same results. My mother still held out hopes for me, but I had moved on.

"I was thinking the other day, it'd be nice to be a telephone lineman," I finally told my mother and her friends one day over coffee and cheesecake. "You work outdoors, you meet a lot of people, you get a paycheck every week. Benefits. It sounds so peaceful, you know?"

They stared at me, their bright red lips working in disbelief, their bright red nails tapping the counter.

"That is a very sick idea," my mother said. "You have the imagination of a mosquito or something. Cut down on the nicotine, for goodness sake."

Most of my mother's friends were people who had been in show business for years, people who might have started singing or dancing as children at state fairs or church socials and just never gave up on the hope of making it big. Most of them had other jobs. They worked as cab drivers, secretaries, salespeople, all so they could have evenings and weekends free for their real passion. In the summer of 1973, however, we met an act that was brand new to the stage.

The first one of them we met was Joni, a tall blond woman with broad shoulders and a big laugh. "Are you decent?" she warbled, as she stuck her head in the women's dressing room door at Curly's. Two more bright and shiny blond women tumbled in after her, giggling and squeaking as they came. They were in their 20s and really, sincerely thrilled to be making their show business debut at Curly's Sea Shack, absolutely giddy and delighted about it. They were not beautiful necessarily, but their tall Marge Simpson hairdos and pastel makeup sure made them stand out. And they were so happy, so stupidly, unflinchingly happy, that it kind of drew you in. After their noisy entrance, a dark-haired boy of about 17 edged quietly into the room. He was reserved and watchful in a way that could have been reassuring or scary.

"Hi, we're the Meterry Sisters!" Joni said. "Are you Dorothy Harris? Gosh, we've been fans of yours since we were little! You played at the Palindrome when we were just tiny girls. That's a little club near us, back in Metairie. Little Julie barely kept her eyes open through your show, didn't you, hon? She was just a tiny baby."

The smallest and chubbiest one scrunched up her face in a smile. "I did love that worm!" she squeaked in a tiny, deeply Southern voice.

But Joni wasn't done. "I guess you noticed—everyone does—that our name is Meterry and we come from Metairie, Louisiana! Our dad didn't plan it or anything—it just happened!" They all laughed themselves silly, except the boy.

If a human could growl, that's what my mother would have been doing as she took them in from her corner of the dressing room. Joni cocked her head a little while catching her breath, as if she had picked up on my mother's attitude, like a canny prey animal sensing danger, but then plowed on anyway.

"Well, I'm Joni, this is Jenny, and Julie—"

"And Jeee-mmy?" my mother said, looking at the boy and imitating Joni's Southern accent.

"David," he said, in a deep, low voice that held a hint of menace.

"He's our brother," Joni said. "He's just here to help us bring our stuff in, then he'll let all us girls alone." She turned to me. I was lying on the floor reading "True Crime" magazine. "Who're you, honey?"

My mother had now turned back to the mirror and continued revising her makeup. "That's Ginger. She's not in the show. Leave her alone."

There were practice rooms and larger dressing areas in the club's basement, but the main dressing rooms were wrapped like a horseshoe around the band's niche at the back of the stage. The women's dressing room was on the left if you were facing the stage and the men's on the right, separated by a curtain that ran perpendicular to the stage. I liked to sit on a chair or on the floor and listen to the stories being told on either side of the curtain. One old favorite was the tale of Hap Hapsburg, a banjo player. He was a study in lifelessness: sandy haired, medium height, pale and quiet. And although banjoes were not a terribly popular instrument at that time, he had managed to build a faithful audience that flocked to his shows. His fans included the wealthy daughter of the owner of a chain of Midwestern department stores. Like so many others, she had come to New York for the excitement. She must have missed something about the slower rhythms of St. Louis, though, because she fell in love with Hap, waiting for him after his shows and learning enough about the banjo to ask him questions that actually got him talking. No one believed it when word got around that they had married and that he had moved into her Park Avenue apartment. A small investigative unit—made up of my mother, Melanie, the woman who played the glasses, and a ventriloquist named Squirt—was dispatched to check out the facts. They spent days loitering around the stylish building where he was supposed to live, trying to see if they would run into him. They made friends with a couple of the building's doormen, who had decided they were harmless. Finally, one day Hap appeared, coming around the corner and mumbling to himself, apparently on his way home.

"He was just as boring and dreary as ever," my mother insisted in her telling of the story. "Just really well dressed." Hap invited them up to his apartment, seven spacious rooms, each one more magnificent than the next.

"And an elevator that opened up and—boom—you're in his apartment," Squirt said.

After the tour, Hap gave them a banjo concert, beginning with an old favorite, "The World Is Waiting for the Sunrise." The three investigators had sat docilely on a silk velvet sofa, listening to Hap "just like old times," Melanie said. They came home bemused but excited. The moral of the story was clear: Success can come in mysterious ways, but if you stick with show business long enough, you will achieve it somehow.

Another story that would be retold for years unfolded that afternoon, when the Meterry Sisters, like my mother and the other performers, had come to the club to rehearse, kibbitz or just get out of the midday sun. On stage, a juggler named Sarto the Magnificent was tossing around some clubs that would be lit as torches when he did his act. After the Meterry Sisters had said hello and were warily edging past my mother further into the dressing room, we suddenly heard some loud thuds from the stage and then shouting. When we got outside, we saw Sarto lying face down in the middle of the stage, clutching his chest. Apparently the clubs had all been in the air when Sarto suddenly grabbed his chest and fell to the floor. The clubs came raining down on him and around him, like children racing to comfort an injured parent. Curly, the gnomelike man who owned the club, told everyone that he had learned CPR from his cousin, who was an ambulance driver. He pushed Sarto onto his back and began slamming his fists on Sarto's chest as if he were hammering in roofing nails. In the silenced club, you could hear Sarto's weak voice pleading, "Stop, stop."

An ambulance came and all of us—Curly, my mom and me, my father, who had been playing cards with the drummer, several other members of the band, all of whom seemed to have toothpicks in their mouths, the Meterry Sisters and their creepy brother, the surly bartender, and a Hawaiian dancer named Nailani—stood in the parking lot and watched as the EMTs loaded Sarto onto a stretcher. They were getting ready to move him into the back when a silver Jaguar XKE with the convertible roof open pulled into the parking lot. It was long and sleek, like something out of British science fiction. Like flowers turning to the sun after weeks of rain, the entire group shifted its attention to the Jaguar. The driver's door opened and Larry Davenport emerged wearing Ray Bans and flashing a smile that was both flirty and charmingly self-deprecating. He scanned the crowd, looking increasingly worried as he noticed the ambulance, but then he smiled when he saw my father.

"Mr. Harris!" he said, opening his arms in greeting.

"Sonny boy!" my father yelled, walking over and throwing his arms around him. My father's reserved pseudo-British style was such a contrast to Larry's buoyant insouciance that the two had a running joke about being father and son.

"You're looking posh, old man," Larry said, lightly punching my father in the arm.

"So good of you to say, Junior," my father said. He mussed Larry's hair with fatherly affection, and Larry made a good-natured attempt not to look annoyed.

On the other side of the car, a small rubbery face emerged and surveyed the crowd. It was Herbie Hughes, a diminutive comedian with a bullet-shaped head. He had gotten his own toehold on fame when he appeared once on the "Ed Sullivan Show." He often was the opening act for Larry when he performed around the country. He came over and joined us. My family and Larry were standing together talking while the rest of the crowd stood in a shy, respectful semi-circle around Larry.

"Where are we, Upper Slobovia?" Herbie asked Larry. He was right: The small crowd's awe and adulation for Larry were so great it was as if a crown prince had arrived in a small peasant village to offer his gratitude to a sheep herding family that had once taken him in as a lost stranger during a snowstorm.

"Herbie," Larry said, "I want you to meet the Harrises, a very talented family who are old friends of mine. Dorothy, my beauty!" He leaned in and kissed my mother, who smiled as if she were indulging a child.

"Ginger," he said, turning to give me a kiss on the cheek. "Still breaking hearts?"

Herbie frowned as he ran his eyes over my head-to-toe statement in black. He leaned sideways toward Larry, tilting until it seemed he must surely fall over, then stopping just before he did. Speaking in a stage whisper out of the side of his mouth, he said to Larry, "When you say breaking hearts, do you mean lit-er-al-ly?"

"What on earth are you doing here, Larry?" my mother asked.

"I'm doing a few weeks at the Pierpont Hotel in Atlantic City. Something else just fell through and this came up." Atlantic City was less than an hour south of Driftwood. It was still a couple of years before gambling would become legal in Atlantic City, and the once popular seaside resort had settled comfortably into a steep decline. A few of the hotels sometimes featured shows with well-known acts in an attempt to attract vacationers from New York or Philadelphia.

"I'm working with Herbie," Larry added, clapping the comedian on the back. Herbie wiggled his eyebrows and made a rude noise.

"You three have to come see the show. Please, be my guests. When are your days off?"

"We'll come, too, Larry," the middle Meterry sister blurted in a strangled whisper, followed by a loud grunt as the oldest sister elbowed her in the side.

"In the meantime, where's a good place for lunch?" Larry asked, putting his arm around my father and steering us out of the parking lot. In answer to Larry's question, Herbie looked around and said, "The next town over?"

Behind us, the crowd sighed as Larry moved away. They turned around and noticed that the ambulance was gone. It would turn out that Sarto had only had a massive attack of indigestion. He would spend the rest of the summer happily juggling flaming clubs without setting himself or anyone else on fire. My family and the visitors went to lunch at a fairly fancy place overlooking the ocean. With every meal, you got great Parker House rolls, served warm so the butter ran off them, the kind of thing that could still delight you when you were 15. My father was not yet having an affair, and I had no idea that the entire summer was about to go up in flames.

Chapter 5

My mother watched the Meterry Sisters from backstage with great interest on their first night on stage. They dressed in matching pastel sequined evening gowns and sang cheerful, old-fashioned songs about their guy and roses and sunsets. Stuff like that.

"Unbelievable," my mother crowed. "Corniest act I've ever seen. This is the 1970s, but nobody knew it on the turnip truck they fell off of."

I was staring at myself in the mirror, something I liked to do. "Time to quit the business, I'd say," I told her cheerfully. "Get a real job."

Usually she ignored me, but something made her stop that night and come over. She sat next to me at the counter and talked to my reflection. "Ginger, I'm just not that kind of person. Your father isn't either. To work at a nine-to-five job, day after day, retire at 65, die six months later. No, it would kill us. You always see people making a fuss over some ancient performer who's still out there, like they're brave or virtuous, but it's the work that keeps them young. Keeps them alive. If you love certainty, then you can be the stable one in the family. Be a big success in an office, marry a successful man. Get your dad and me out of hock. Maybe you'll like it, but it would kill the two of us. So you get to support us in retirement, kid."

Like most kids, I tended to think of myself as just another wheel on my parents' jalopy, but during your teenage years you begin to hold them at arm's length and inspect them. Many of us start to wonder what part we are going to continue to play in the rambling road show that is our parents' life. When my mother said this, that she could envision me remaining the solid metal pole that would hold up their brightly colored tent forever, she was only confirming a sickening suspicion I had had for a long time: that she believed I had signed up for a life term of being their factotum. But I didn't have long to dwell on her beliefs.

Outside, we heard the Meterry Sisters begin to sing "God Bless America," a rousing anthem to patriotism. My mother's chair tumbled over as she jumped from it and ran to the curtain to see what they were doing.

"Look what the hell they're doing!" she shouted. "Look what the hell they're doing! They are singing 'God Bless America.' Ginger, do you hear what they're singing?"

"'God Bless America?'"

"People in the audience are standing and… I think they're marching or something. The little fat sister is waving a flag. You know what I gotta do now? I gotta follow the glory of our country with frickin' 'Glowworm.'"

There is a very strict order to how shows are presented. The general idea is that you save the best for last. You don't want a quiet act to follow a strong one. Once you get people laughing or crying, they typically get too restless to settle down and watch the next act play an instrument or tap dance. It's just too sedate by contrast. So, you want to get people's attention by starting a show with an act that is fun and interesting but not the best thing you've got. You would have thought that the Meterry Sisters were a good example of fun and interesting but not too interesting. So it would have seemed reasonable to follow them with several acts like my mother's, because a xylophone player was very unusual and people really did get a kick out of that worm. Although Curly mixed things up now and then, the last act was usually my dad, with his comedy magic. That was because once people relaxed and started laughing, came up on stage to get their balloons or participate in tricks, it was hard to get them to quiet down and pay attention to a more serious act. That's where you get the expression "a hard act to follow." Once someone has done something extraordinary, they expect nothing less from the next person. The Meterry Sisters had broken the rules by using "God Bless America" in an opening act, because once people get all riled up and patriotic—once they start marching, for pity's sake—it would be hard for someone else to calm them down and get them to watch a dancing worm. That night, the sisters, who really were not a show-stopping act most of the time, broke down the established order and would leave my mother struggling to reclaim the audience's attention.

"Me or those sisters," my mother seethed, peering out onto the stage. "Somebody's gotta go."

I walked down to the beach during my parents' part of the show that night. It was something I did often because I had seen the acts a thousand times. I liked the beach best at night, when the only sound you could hear was the crashing of the waves.

"Are you going to be a dancer? You're very graceful."

I had been lying on my back with my eyes closed, but now I sat up to see a young, dark-haired guy sitting near me. Although the lights of the boardwalk were very bright, much of his face was still in shadows. He had a deep voice that came out in a kind of masculine whisper.

"A dancer? No. Go away."

"Are you going to be a musician like your mother?"

"My mother's not a musician. Not really."

"I'm going to be a musician. I play the cello."

"Who the heck are you?"

"David Meterry. You met my sisters. I was there, too."

"Oh. The daughters of the American Revolution."

He sighed. "They mean well," he said.

"Everybody does, don't they?" I looked over and assessed him. His hair was shorter than most guys wore it then and he wore casual but neat clothes. He would have been called "clean cut" in 1973. But there was still something dangerous about him. As if there were a lot of strong feelings underneath the calm exterior. It was unclear whether it would be a good idea to find out what they were. But that was fine, because I was already up to my ears in interesting people. No need to add more.

"So, what's your story?" I asked, to be polite. "Your parents are dead and you kids are all hanging together? You hear that one a lot."

There was a long pause. "Well, yes, actually," he finally said. "They were killed in a car accident. Last year. My father was a band leader. The Meterry Music Meisters."

I didn't really know what to say to that, so we just sat for a while, looking at the water and fidgeting.

"Where would you go if you were going to run away?" he finally asked.

"Run away? I don't know. I come from New York. That's where people run away to."

"Come on, there has to be somewhere." He had that very quiet voice, but a very confident and self-assured manner. He really was almost scary. "Don't you have any imagination?"

"I have imagination." I thought for a while, trying to prove I had imagination. "Okay, I guess I'd go to Paris. That's somewhere worth going even if you start out in New York."

"What would you do there?"

"Be a telephone lineman."

"What?"

"Look, everyone gives me a hard time about this. I just want to be someone who repairs telephone lines, or something like that. It's just a thing to do. Honest, simple work. It's just a normal life."

I guess I stumped him with that one, because we were quiet again for a while.

"So, where are you from," I finally asked. "Paducah? Biloxi? Kutztown?"

"You're kind of a bitch, you know?" he said.

I smiled happily out at the water. "It's a family tradition."

He leaned in close to me. "It suits you," he whispered. He kissed me gently on the cheek, then got up and walked back toward the boardwalk.

Chapter 6

It was about two weeks later that I found my dad making out with Julie Meterry—the little fat Meterry sister—in the practice room. He apparently knew I had seen him. For days after that, he desperately tried to make eye contact with me. He even tried to get me interested in new balloon animals—I believe he was attempting something revolutionary with an octopus—but I avoided him as much as possible.

For the summer, we had rented a tiny bungalow filled with dilapidated beach furniture that was about seven blocks from the boardwalk. My room was barely big enough for a twin bed. The kitchen—a half-size refrigerator and two hot plates—ran along one wall of the living room and there was sand in everything, but I loved it there. It was cozy and it smelled of the ocean. And if it was far from perfect that was fine, because we were just visiting. That's why I didn't mind traveling too much, something we continued to do for large parts of the year. If life on the road was ever awful, you were always on your way to somewhere else. There was always hope for the next place.

"Curly told me the business isn't the same as it was last year," my mother said at dinner one night. "It hasn't been the same as the year before for a few years now. Things are changing, Ted!"

My father grunted as he brushed his moustache and stared into space, pushing his spaghetti around on his plate. This was pretty typical dinner repartee for our family. My mother shouted out declarative sentences and my father grunted.

"I can't believe how big the ocean is!" or "What were the neighbors thinking with those curtains?" or "It's disgusting that the new accordion player has six fingers on her right hand!"

I tried to slither out of my chair and into another room as soon as possible without being noticed.

So that night, as soon as I could, I went to sit on our miniscule screened-in front porch, curled up in a big pink wicker chair. Across the way, an old man watched a ballgame on a small black and white TV he had brought out onto the porch. I could hear the rise and fall of the announcers' voices and the surge of the crowd's roar. At some point my father went out for a walk. He had been doing that a lot lately. What was even weirder was that my mother also went for a long walk. When she finally came home, she sat next to me on the porch.

"So, how'd you like the show tonight?" she asked.

"I didn't see it. I went to the beach."

"Oh, sounds like fun. Whaddja do?"

"Picked up a sailor."

She grabbed me by the arm, hurting just a little. "I'm not a person you jerk around, Ginger. I don't know why you haven't learned that yet."

She lit a cigarette and waved it around a while. "I can't wait to be famous, you know?" she said. Larry's plans for her had clearly had an impact.

Like devoted cultists, all show people believe devoutly in the Big Break. But there had been peaks and valleys in my parents' road to fame and fortune before, so I was going to wait and see on this one. I continued to examine my fingernails, which were painted with purple glitter polish.

"Meanwhile, those women, the Bitsy Sisters, they're driving me crazy. They natter like chipmunks," she said. "It's making me, I don't know, nauseous or something. I just don't feel right this summer."

She kept looking at me, sighing heavily, waiting for me to join in.

"I don't know how much longer this is going to last, the way we live," she said. "Thank God I don't have to worry too much about that, since Larry's getting me in front of the right people. But Dad, I don't know what he'll do then. Or what will happen to any of us if it all falls through. Which it won't." She stared at me a while, then took a puff and exhaled the smoke loudly. "The world is changing, yes, it is!"

I picked up the *Driftwood Journal* from a stack of newspapers on the porch and began to read about preparations for CrabFest 1973, which the paper said would take place in August.

"Listen, your highness," she finally erupted. "I'm on the verge of fame and I can't afford any, shall we say, domestic trouble. I'm not going to put up with that, oh no I'm not."

She stared at me as if her head was glued in place. "I can't afford to be distracted or… embarrassed… right now. And I don't know how I'm going to keep the family together when I make it big. What do you think we should do about it?"

"About what?"

She waved her hand around in annoyance. "When I become famous, it's going to be very important for me to keep my family together. That's going to be a challenge, don't you think?"

But I was already absorbed once again in CrabFest 1973, which the paper said would feature local crabs, known as Driftwood Devils. She slammed her cigarette out in a conch shell on the floor and lit another one.

"All right, let me spell it out for you. I need your help. You're surprised that I would ask that, aren't you, since I'm usually the one who takes care of everything? Well, I'm obviously not going to give you a lot of authority, but I could use someone to do a little espionage for me."

She stared at me as if she had made a very provocative remark, but I had years of experience ignoring her. She tried again.

"Have you noticed anything unusual, Ginger, you know what I mean? Like the world is just a little off? Like we have a problem we need to attend to? Something I need to settle once and for all before I'm appearing on 'Dean Martin' and can't be associated with scandal? Something I'm going to put an end to right now?"

I was still looking at the paper. There would also be a bikini contest at CrabFest, I learned.

"All right," she continued. "You're making me beg, I'll beg." She began to whisper, even though we were alone. The next porch was just an arm's length away, it was true, but on both sides the houses were rented by older couples from Philadelphia who went to bed early, and I could see that the guy across the way was snoozing over his ballgame, his head resting on his chest.

"I have reason to believe we have a problem," she hissed. "You don't know what I'm referring to, do you, even though you're such a smarty pants?" She shook her head at me smugly. "I have reason to believe your father may have a crush on someone here. Which is cute, but not something I can be thinking about when I'm going for my audition with Dean Martin. I need a nice stable home life behind me when I'm making it big. No nonsense, no funny stuff."

Thinking of my father and the little fat Meterry sister in the practice room, I dropped the plastic glass I was holding, which bounced loudly and spilled Dr. Pepper on both of us. "A crush? Why would you think that?"

"A woman knows," she said, wiping us off with a dish towel that she had tucked into the belt on her dress. "You wouldn't know, you're not a woman yet."

She pulled her chair even closer, exhaling cigarette smoke onto me. "I hope you understand the severity of the situation. Of course, it's nothing, just some flirting maybe. Because I would not put up with more than that! But if I were to lose my patience and the two of us were to break up? My big break could be jeopardized. Divorce is so unseemly. And our family, I don't know what would happen. Life as we know it is over. No more happy family! No more summers at the beach for you, Toots. Your magical childhood? Pfft! So, we have to work together, you understand me? We have to be partners, you and I."

"What are you saying?" She was holding on to me with a sticky, Dr. Pepper-stained hand. I tried to pull away from her.

"I need your help," she hissed, leaning closer. "I need your assistance in this very important matter. I have some very important opportunities ahead of me and I don't have time to be worrying about your father's… peccadillos."

I waited a moment to shake off the idea of my father's peccadillos and the memory of him and little fat Julie slobbering on each other in the rehearsal room at Curly's. And I tried to fight off the sickening fear that had begun to stir as this conversation went on.

Underneath my cool, calm exterior was the terrified concern that all of our lives were built on shaky ground. I had worries about their acts, their show business career and even the entire little niche of the business they called their own. I watched the audiences when they worked and, although many seemed to like their performances, I could also see enough occasional snickering and eye rolling to worry me.

I wondered a lot about their marriage, too, about whether it was really all right to spend so much time making impatient remarks to each other. But until I'd found out about my dad's affair, I would have thought I just didn't know enough to get how adult relationships worked. Once again, it was an example of what kids do when their parents' world doesn't make sense: Make up a reasonable justification so you can stop thinking about it. When I felt a hint of panic about our future, I reminded myself that I was just a snarky teenager. I could have an opinion and it could be wrong and that was fine. But I had believed *they* had full faith in the lives we were living. In my mind, their unity and their confidence were the flimsy bits of safety net holding us together, the driving force that kept us going despite all odds. They must know something I didn't, right? But if my mother was actually asking for help now—if her certainty was disappearing— then I knew we must really be in trouble. And she didn't even know that the problem was a lot larger than my dad's crush on someone. If I really knew more than she did, that was trouble. As we had that conversation that night, with the sounds of the Phillies game and the smell of Dr. Pepper wafting around us, I knew it was time to be afraid.

"I don't know what you're asking," I told her. My mother was so close it seemed we were sitting in the same chair, and I was almost sure I could feel her long false eyelashes scrape against my face.

"I want you to find out if it's true. I want you to watch him like a hawk and tell me what you see. And her—her especially. She's the key to the thing, isn't she? I can't do it, you see. I have to be discreet. But I have to know what's up."

"Wait a minute, you don't even know what's happening. You're not even sure who he's supposed to be interested in."

I suppose my voice was rising along with my panic, because the man across the street woke up, turning down the sound on the seventh inning and peering across at us momentarily. She put a finger to her lips while nodding her head. "Oh, yes I do," she whispered. The words hung in the air like puffs of cigarette smoke between us.

"You do?" I wracked my brains trying to imagine when she could have seen my father and Julie. Had she noticed them that night in the rehearsal room?

"Yes, I do know who it is, my dear," she said at last. "It's Yolanda, from that 'Lady of Spain' act. Reynolds and Yolanda. I've suspected that for a while."

I could barely contain my laughter. Yolanda—a tall, big-boned, sexy and imposing woman—was part of a dance act that was playing that summer at Curly's. My parents had been booked on shows with them often in the past. Yolanda couldn't have been more different from fat little Julie. If he was smitten with Julie, he would never have looked twice at Yolanda.

"Dad and Yolanda? I find that really unbelievable," I told her through relieved hiccupping snorts of laughter. "I'm sure it's not true." We had known Reynolds and Yolanda for quite a while, but I had never suspected anything. Or found my father making out with Yolanda.

"You watch him for a while, you'll see. And that's your job this summer, to watch him. Don't just do it for me. Do it for our family. If we can't set this right, it's going to be a real horror show."

*

Picture my father and Julie screaming loudly, their eyes and mouths wide with terror. My father's face had an unnatural flush to it and little bits of spittle were threatening to spill over Julie's lower lip. Then they disappeared, sucked into a vortex and down the chute.

It was the next day, and they were riding the roller coaster at a boardwalk amusement park, like two kids on a date, as if there was no one else in the world who might see them. After that they went on the bumper cars, and Julie turned out to be a pretty psychotic driver, slamming repeatedly into the side of a car driven by an obnoxious 10-year-old and nearly bringing an aggressive teenage driver to tears. Then they tried to win a prize, squirting water into a clown's mouth, and when they failed completely at that they gleefully began squirting water at each other.

I laughed then; I couldn't help myself. My father was dressed like a dapper young man from the 1920s, in pastel linen, while Julie wore a cotton print dress. I wore dark glasses and a Phillies hat with my hair stuffed into it so no one would recognize me. I was following them because my mother had asked me to keep an eye on him and his new crush, she just had the wrong girl. I thought it was wise to watch them at least some of the time to prevent my mother from stumbling on the affair he was actually having.

After the clown booth, my dad bought Julie cotton candy. He accidentally got some in her hair as he was paying for it, so she took some and rubbed it into his hair, then they tumbled into a giggling cotton candy food fight. They looked ridiculously happy and something like… in love. My father looked less distant and more boyish than I'd ever seen him.

Then I turned and saw my mother, heading straight toward them and looking lethal. I was closer, though, so I raced over to them. "Look sad, look sad, look sad!" I hissed. They stared, stunned to see me, not completely sure who I was in my clever disguise and bewildered by what I was saying. "Mom!" I whisper/shouted. Their faces immediately fell and we all turned wide and weirdly depressed eyes toward her, trying to appear innocent.

"There you are," she said, sweeping up to us. "I couldn't find you anywhere. What are you doing?"

We all stood stupidly for a minute. "We wanted to take Ginger on some rides," Julie finally blurted out.

"Rides?" My mother frowned, then swiveled her head to take in the rumbling, squealing, rattling array of amusement rides that were whizzing by her and over her head.

"Oh, yeah. I did that with her once. I didn't think you liked that stuff." She stopped then and focused on my father. After the food fight and all those rides, his tie was horizontal, one of his jacket pockets was turned out and his hair stood up straight from his head.

"What happened to you?" my mother asked, squinting. "You look like my Uncle Waldo's Cousin Fritz."

More silence. "Mrs. Harris," Julie piped in. "Your daughter is such a… charming girl."

All three of us turned to her in disbelief. "Thank you, I'm sure," my mother said. "By the way, who the heck are you?"

"I'm Julie Meterry. One of the Meterry Sisters?"

My mother smiled a sickening smile. "My worst nightmare come true." She yanked me toward her. "Thanks for your interest, dear, but I don't want my child growing up to be an airline stewardess. I'd prefer she didn't spend time with you. I still have hope for her." She turned to my father. "Unlike you."

Then she pulled me away from them, down the boardwalk. "The one good thing you can say about those women, you know your father would never be interested in one of them!"

"Absolutely not!" I practically shouted.

Then my mother stopped short and caught sight of something on the beach. I followed her gaze and saw the dancer Yolanda sunning herself on a towel. She was truly stunning in a wine-red bikini. People insist that the cadaverous models in Vogue are the standard that little girls are forced to aspire to, but Yolanda had not gotten that memo. She wasn't fat, certainly, but rounded and robust and proud of it.

My mother's face had turned pasty and her lips had flattened into a firm line. "Since last spring, when we were booked with them in Trenton, your father's been hanging around her like a yutz," she said, her voice a harsh whisper. "She's really a Jewish girl from Forest Hills, I happen to know that. Not this senorita she pretends to be. She probably thinks she has Ted wrapped around her finger, but she doesn't know my Ginger's on the case. She has no idea what's going on, does she?"

"None at all," I told her.

Chapter 7

The funny thing about my mother's request was that I was already an accomplished spy of sorts. On some streets in Driftwood there was a sandy strip that ran behind the yards of the houses, sort of like an alleyway. I liked to let myself out at night and prowl along these alleyways. There was usually a certain amount of scrub brush and tall beach grass that had grown up along the way, and that foliage and the darkness gave me cover. I wasn't up to anything bad, I just liked to see how other people lived. The houses were mainly one-story bungalows or very small Cape Cods. You usually entered through a screened-in porch, then came to a living room and a small dining area, with a kitchen or kitchenette behind them. There would be two or three bedrooms along the sides of the house, and as the houses got nicer there would also be a small back porch.

I got to know a lot of families from afar during those summers. There was one family with twins, and there were two little red tricycles sitting on their back porch. One of the kids seemed to be a good sleeper, but the mom was often up, even in the wee hours of the night, walking the other one around. Was she quietly, secretly thinking about how much she liked the other one better? Or did those long nights together form a bond between them that the other one missed out on? A few houses down, there was an older couple who sat on their back porch each night, in what I'd have to call a companionable silence. They didn't read or drink or smoke and rarely talked. They seemed simply to be listening to the faint sound of the waves and maybe reviewing the day in their minds. They were one of my biggest challenges because I worried that they might easily hear me, rustling by in the bushes near them. But they never seemed to notice, or if they did they ignored me, perhaps dismissing me as a small animal on her night rounds. No matter how much time I spent in their company, or how alert I was to their moves or moods, I couldn't discern anything but contentment around them. I wondered how they had gotten there. Had they spent years fighting, then finally figured out what the problem was and dispatched with it? Or had they started out happy together and just spent a lifetime that way, with no need to say too much because they knew all about each other already? Questions like these kept me watching other people's houses at night. It was doubly interesting because even though my family was spending the summer at the beach, we weren't really on vacation, since my parents were there to work. If not for the sand and the sea, we might as well have been at a convention in Scranton. The people were not just different from us because they had conventional routines, but because they had a chance to escape their routines, if only temporarily, and that idea interested me. In my family, show business followed us everywhere.

I have to admit that fairly shortly after we met them, I started scouting the Meterrys' house. It was about three blocks closer to the beach than ours, so a little bit more expensive to rent. That made me wonder if the sisters weren't doing pretty well in their relatively new act. The first time I went there, I was battling my way through some particularly thick bushes, only to burst out and discover them all sitting on their back porch. They didn't see me, so I quickly lay down on the sand beneath the bush and listened to their voices. I couldn't quite hear what they were saying, but there was a lot of feminine murmuring and laughing, with occasional rumbles of David's deep voice. Then I heard moving around and assumed they were going inside, but a moment later I heard Joni's strong voice say, "5, 6, 7, 8," and they were singing. It was so surprising that my head snapped up and got wedged between some low-slung branches as I tried to see what was up. Joni had a guitar and David had a violin, and all the sisters were singing a brisk but somewhat melancholy song about home or a bird or an old flannel shirt or whatever folk tunes are about.

When it was over they didn't laugh or talk or slap each other five or all that stuff people do when they've accomplished any old thing; they just sat together in silence. I stuck my head out a little farther because the quiet was unnerving, demanding some response, as if the TV sound had died and it was time to give the set a slap on the side or fiddle with the antenna. But they were just sitting there, looking if not content then at least as peaceful as that older couple did in their silence. What was even weirder was that they seemed to do this often, perhaps even as much as every night, based on my observations.

It finally struck me that this might have been a song that their parents had taught them, or that had been special to their family in some way. It made me think about what it must be like to lose a parent, or two all at once like that. It must take a while to get over the idea that the parent will still be doing familiar things and waiting for you in familiar places. It must shift your sense of yourself, as well. When you're a kid, most of your job is just showing up and following along. When a parent just disappears one day, there's a whole world you'll now have to navigate. You have to decide if you're going to find a new way—a new leader—to follow or if you're going to thrash along through the vast world on your own. I had to hand it to the Meterrys since they seemed to be trying to do the latter, in their own hick way. Figuring out the world on their own. If I was in that spot, I was thinking at the time, I'd also rather be prepared to swim than grab on to the first boat that happened by.

On another late night, the weird thing happened again. I was lying in my bed, reading *Anna Karenina*, because despite the impression I might give I was actually a very smart and well-read kid with precocious literary tastes. After a while I realized that there had been a light tapping on the screen door for a while, but I had thought it was water dripping somewhere or mice working their way into the kitchen.

"Hello?" a voice finally called.

It was the woman who had come to our apartment, the dark well-dressed one. "Hello, Ginger," she said, in a very formal voice when I finally came to the door.

She seemed nice and very well put together, confident. Something about her reminded me of how much I don't know about the lives of ordinary people.

"How did you know we were here? How do you know where we live?"

She sighed and gave me a hard stare. "I – I know Dorothy very well. I've known her forever. I know how to find her when I need to."

She certainly didn't look like a fan, although it was possible that xylophone aficionados came from all walks of life. I was wary, though. There were often strange people—usually men but occasionally women—who hung around trying to become friends with the performers. They could be dangerous. Once a woman sprayed Raid at a singer she insisted was having an affair with her husband, and it turned out that the woman with the Raid hadn't even been married. "Mildreds," my mother called them, because I think she thought the name had a disheartened sound that gave it insult value.

"May I ask if you gave her my message?" this woman asked. "From last time?"

"Yes, but she's a very busy person. You may wait a while to hear from her."

"Oh, I know that. Well, here's another note for her, with my number. It's quite important that she call me. Goodbye, Ginger."

She nodded, looking quite friendly, and then got into a car that she'd parked in front of our house.

Her visit made me antsy, since I couldn't figure her out, so I went to the beach. When you have very hard-working parents, you learn to become extremely self-sufficient. And spending time alone was not always such a bad thing. I enjoyed my own company.

David snuck up on me as I was hunting for shells. "Do you want to go swimming?" he asked. I ignored him. He followed me along like a dog for a while as I squinted at the sand, looking for new specimens. Most of what you find on the Jersey shore are mollusk shells, but you can also find shells for hard and soft shell clams, blue mussel, bay scallops and razor clams. I really was a big reader and it was fun to see the world in person after so much time coming to know it in books. For all our travels, I spent a great deal of my time backstage.

David was watching me speculatively. "I bet you don't know how to swim," he said after a while. "Living in an apartment in New York City. Parents kind of busy all the time. You don't, do you?" I could hear the light Louisiana twang in his voice when he made the classic out-of-towner's mistake of calling it "New York City." If you were a New Yorker, there was only one New York, so no qualifier was necessary.

I stood up and stretched. "I just don't do it, all right? No need to analyze why. I just don't."

He stepped closer to me. He had a habit of getting too deep into someone else's space. "Why don't you decide not to be that person?" he asked. "Just for tonight?"

"What does that mean?"

"Listen, you weren't born with dyed-black hair and a bad attitude. You had to choose to dress that way and act that way and be that way. But if you want to try something different, like swimming, you can just decide that for tonight you're not going to be that girl. The one who's too cool to do it. You can decide to be different from the person you are every day. To try something you're not good at. See what it's like."

I ignored him and went back to hunting for shells. "Are you going to be a cellist?" I asked after a while. People love talking about themselves, that much I knew for sure, so I hoped it would distract him from nosing around in my life.

"Yes, in a string quartet. I hope."

"Do you make any money at that?"

"Some. But money's not the only thing that's important."

"Ha! Do you have a few hours to hear my life story?"

"Yes," he said.

I sat down, suddenly very tired and a little dizzy. "Well, anyway, money's important to some people." I rubbed my eyes hard, pushing the heels of my hands into them. I was trying hard not to cry, but it finally overcame me.

"You know," I finally said between choking sobs, "my father's fooling around with your sister."

"Which one?"

"My father is Ted Harris. The guy with the balloon act?"

"No, Ginger, which sister?"

"Oh. The little fat one."

"Julie." He was clearly surprised. "Well, I'm really sorry."

"It's okay," I said, crying almost uncontrollably. "No harm done." I fell over onto the sand and curled up in a ball.

He dropped to the ground and put his arm around me. "There, is that what your mom does when you cry?"

"She takes an Excedrin."

"Ah, a health food nut. Let's talk about Ginger, then. What's your favorite food, Ginger?" He stroked my hair as he talked.

"Corned beef hash," I sobbed.

"With the fried egg on top or not?"

"No, just out of the can. But cooked."

"But cooked, that's good. What's your favorite song?"

"'Stairway to Heaven.'"

"Oh, my God, what drivel. Like a knife to my heart. Okay, what do you want to be when you grow up?"

"The most ordinary thing you can be without dying of boredom."

"So many choices. Why set your sights so low?"

"Low? You mean it's better to be a colorful loser than contented but... ordinary?"

He thought a moment. "Probably."

I snorted. "You haven't been around show business long enough. All right, we'll see then. We'll meet in 10 years and see who's happier."

"Deal," he said. "And now, we're going swimming."

"No. No, no. You can't swim in the ocean at night. There's a law. Or a statute. And there are creatures in there that you can't see. Especially at night. Jellyfish and sharks and sardines and minnows. No."

"They let us swim at the Lido Motel. My sisters and me. There's a pool."

"You can't swim there at night."

"Yeah, I know the guy. Come on."

David, who could have played the charming serial killer in a TV movie, had a habit of knowing a guy. He was extremely quiet and yet a great schmoozer, both at the same time. I think people were intrigued by how funny and smart he turned out to be once he actually spoke. So for about two hours that night David tried to teach me to swim.

Motels—or motor hotels—were invented in the 1920s when people first began to drive to a vacation. Like many of its kind, the

Lido was a two-story L-shaped building with rows of rooms whose doors faced a patio that surrounded a pool. There were a few lights on in the rooms, but the curtains were closed, so the patio was mostly in darkness, except for the dim glow of sconces between each pair of room doors. David disappeared for a moment and then the underwater lights in the pool came on, giving the pool and patio an unearthly shimmering radiance. See, this part is not so bad, I thought. When I was in an unpleasant situation, I liked to stop and remind myself of the good things whenever possible, to maintain my native optimism.

I wore one of his sister Jenny's bathing suits with a T-shirt over it because I didn't have a suit of my own. The lesson wasn't terribly successful. First, I tried pushing myself off from the sides of the pool. I would glide beautifully for a few feet, then sink straight down. Then, David held me up as I lay on my back, but when he took his arms away I sank. And screamed a little. Everything I tried, eventually I would sink. But that was all right. It was true, what David had said. It was interesting to decide just for one night not to be that person who refused to swim. To see what it was like to be a new you. Like a small vacation, knowing you can always go home if you felt like it.

We took the long way home, heading down from the Lido to the boardwalk, then back up the lengthy blocks to my house. Along the way, we passed a phone booth on Sea Breeze Avenue, the wide shopping street that was one block up from the beach. It seemed to be glowing as we approached, then we could see that there was a woman inside, wearing a long gold dress. She was speaking urgently to someone and had a dreamy, satisfied smile on her face. Every once in a while she would flinch in a way that appeared to be a giggle.

As we got closer, there was no mistaking the heavily made-up Cleopatra eyes and ruby-red lips. I walked up to the booth and pulled open the stiff accordion-fold doors.

"What are you doing?" I yelled. It was true that there was no phone in our bungalow, but it was about 2 in the morning and I couldn't imagine who she'd be calling. Everyone we usually called was already here in Driftwood, staying in rentals without phones.

"Shut up and go away," my mother said. "I'm talking to the coast."

In show business parlance, in New York at least, the idea of "talking to the coast" held a grave importance. It referred to the West Coast, or Hollywood, and if you were talking to someone there you were surely setting the stage for a chance to move out there to become a movie or television star.

I stepped back instinctively and let the door snap shut. My mother turned her back and said something in a laughingly apologetic voice. It was true that it was three hours earlier in California, but I still couldn't understand what she was doing here on a street corner in Driftwood in the middle of the night, holding a conversation with what must have been a very good friend, based on her lazy smile and a flirtatious manner that I could discern even with her back turned to me.

"Hey, Ginger." I remembered that David was there. He was gently pulling me away from the phone. "Let me show you Cassiopeia."

"Is that some cellist?" I said. I knew better, but I was trying to humor him while I figured out what was wrong with my mother. He was also always trying to teach me interesting new things and I felt it was important to undermine those efforts.

"It's a constellation. It's shaped like a W—or an M I guess, depending how you look at it—and there are five main stars…."

I let him lead me off, and we wandered up the street, heading away from the beach and toward my bungalow, looking for stars. I knew it was a bad time of year to be looking for Cassiopeia, but I needed more time to think about this new hitch in what I continued to hope might just be part of a long road to eventual normalcy.

The next day there was a bunch of wildflowers sitting in a child's beach bucket on our porch steps. A piece of paper attached to the bucket handle with a piece of red yarn said only "For Ginger." Every day after that, a bunch of wildflowers was waiting on the steps, tied with a red string.

Chapter 8

I ended up following half of Driftwood to make sure my mother didn't find out about my father's affair. I followed my father, especially when he was with Julie. I even followed Yolanda some of the time so I could report on her to my mother. If my mother was concentrating on Yolanda, I reasoned, she would never find out about Julie. And Yolanda did not present a danger.

I began to know my father and Julie's patterns, what places they liked to meet and what motels they went to, because they were having a full-blown affair. David and I spent a lot of time walking around in big hats and sunglasses as part of our disguise. I hadn't meant to include him in my reconnaissance missions, but it became unavoidable. One day I followed my dad and Julie to a miniature golf course on the far end of the boardwalk. To avoid detection, I was wearing a baseball hat and a tennis outfit that I had shoplifted from a store called Court and Course. I was pacing up and down on the boardwalk smoking while they hacked away at the ball. Every few seconds I would hear one of Julie's shrieking giggles.

"You look like Woody Allen on holiday," a voice said. It was, of course, David.

"Are you following me?"

"Are you following them?" He tipped his head toward the mini golf course.

"Yes," I hissed. "And you're blowing my cover."

"Your cover?" He gave a kind of interrupted half smile that I wished I knew how to do. "You're in the CIA now?"

"Shut up. I'm keeping an eye on my father and your sister because my mother asked me. I don't need you interfering." We were whispering now, huddled together on a bench facing away from the mini golf, overlooking the beach.

"Your mother knows they're together?" David asked.

"No, it's just part of a bigger plan that I can't really bother explaining to you."

He stopped and considered me for a moment. "Why are you doing it?" he asked. "No reason you have to. That's their problem, not yours."

I sighed. "Listen, things are a little more complicated in my world than in Gingham Curtain, Arkansas."

His lips and his eyes narrowed. Of course he was angry. He was devoted to those moronic sisters and their mythically wonderful childhood. It flickered through my mind that he looked good angry, with the skin of his face drawn tightly over his strong features.

"My parents are holding on to their show biz careers by their fingernails," I finally explained, getting impatient now with his limited grasp of a more challenging world. "I'm not really sure how we pay for rent or food or anything. Most of the time we probably don't. Even as it is, I wouldn't be surprised if they're going to tell me that our next big adventure will be to live in a tunnel in Riverside Park and dig for our meals in garbage cans. They'd try to sell it to me like they sell their acts to an audience. 'How many of your friends live in a park? We have a river view! We can shop in garbage cans outside the best restaurants!'" On the edge of hysteria, I had started throwing my arms around and imitating my parents. David gently put a finger to his lips and I stopped and took a long breath.

"And that's with the two of them together," I finally said, more composed. "If they split up—if my idiot mother leaves him because

74

she finds out or something—there's no chance they can afford two apartments, or two sets of groceries, or me." We both knew I was on the edge of tears again and he waited patiently as I pulled myself together one more time.

"I can't keep their careers together," I finally said, although some of my words might have been nearly sobs. "I don't know how much longer we can all hold our breath in case their careers do come back. This thing with Larry? I don't know, I've given up hoping for miracles. But I can try to hold them together, because everything can't just goddamn fall apart at once." I'm pretty sure the words were just hiccupped gulps at that point.

"Okay, okay, Ginger," David said. "We'll do it. I'll help you. Don't you think it would be more inconspicuous if we were together? Running into you alone way out here, or wherever they go, is a little suspicious. Like you're following them. But if they run into two people, they'll think we were just out hanging around together."

So that's how David and I became a surveillance team. He seemed to like being helpful, and I was not above letting someone help me right at that time. We started out deciding to take some preventive measures. We went to the Clam Shell Motel, where we'd already seen them going to meet one day. It was a slightly concave two-story building that ran along the beach, with parking in back. The office was also in back, in a frigidly air conditioned room that was seemingly wallpapered with the husks of coconuts, brown with scraggly hair hanging from it. Next to the desk, there was a picture of John F. Kennedy made out of very small clam shells. The desk clerk, a motherly looking woman wearing a faded beach cover up, scrutinized us as we came in.

"We don't take hippies here," she said.

I laughed out loud. "You think we're hippies? This is what hippies wear? Black? Hippies don't wear black. Are you out of your mind? Is anyone under 75 a hippie now?" The stress of the summer was clearly starting to get to me.

"Excuse me, ma'am," David said, ignoring my opening banter. He pulled two professional photos out of a manila envelope, one of my dad holding a magic wand in the air and giving a wide-eyed smile and one of Julie in three-quarter profile with a giant pile of hair on her head. I don't know where he got them, but I had gotten used to his surprises. "Have these people ever stayed in your fine motel?"

Asked to participate in what she must have thought was some kind of official inquiry, the woman dropped the attitude immediately. She looked over the pictures and then raised her face to us.

"No, sir," she said. Seeing her overly wide eyes and blank expression, you could tell she definitely knew them but had decided she wasn't supposed to say. She leaned forward slightly, tipping her whole body over the desk. "Are you the police?"

"Are you kidding me?" I said. "First we were hippies—"

"Of course not, ma'am," David said. "Put that thought from your mind right now. It's actually kind of a shameful family tragedy. This gentleman is this young lady's dad." He pointed to me and I smiled smugly. "And he and the pretty lady in this picture have run off together. She was in a convent school, you know. It's a tragedy. They think they're in love, but they're ruining their lives. Do you know what I mean?"

She nodded her head eagerly.

"They're not bad people, just confused," David continued.

"Yes," she muttered, eager to hear the story.

"We want them to come back home, so we're trying to get owners of fine motels like yours to—well, I'm embarrassed to say it—but to refuse to rent rooms to them. We're hoping that will encourage them to stop running around and come back to the bosom of their families."

"The bosom—" I began.

"Oh my, that is sad," the woman said, smiling happily. She looked back and forth at the pictures of the two reprobates, drinking them in. "But this is a very reputable motel, and we can't have scandal here. I definitely won't have them here."

"Thank you so much, ma'am. We're both so grateful to you."

Our next stop was Sharkey's Banana Hut, which was a couple of blocks off the beach and definitely shabbier than the Clam Shell, but just the kind of out of the way place you'd go to conduct an affair, especially if you'd been refused by glamorous places like the Clam Shell. The desk clerk was a guy in his thirties with long shaggy hair and a Blue Oyster Cult T-shirt. The office was purely functional, with hospital green walls and a linoleum desk. It had the burnt rubber smell I knew was marijuana, because Brian the night manager in our apartment building at home was a real pothead.

"My man," the pothead said to David as we walked in.

"How're you doing?" David said. He slapped the photos on the table. "Have you seen these two? I mean, have they stayed here?"

The clerk looked them over and nodded. "Yeah, I think so. About a week ago. Short stay. Couple of hours. You know what I mean. What's wrong with them?"

"Deadbeats. Did they pay?"

The guy shrugged. "Yeah, I don't remember any problem."

"Well, they're our aunt and uncle, and they're completely irresponsible. They've been hopping around towns on the shore this summer, ripping people off. We're trying to save them from themselves, if you know what I mean. So, maybe you're full if they come around again?"

"No problem. I don't want them here. If they stiff me I could get fired." He looked over the pictures once again, his fingers edging them towards him. "Can I keep these?"

"No." I pulled the photos out from under his hand. This storyline was getting too close to reality for me and we didn't need to leave any identification behind.

"Anyway," the guy said, scratching his head as David put the pictures away, "this place is for sale so who knows what will happen next here. Everything in Driftwood seems to be for sale. Lombardo's, Curly's, the Rusty Scupper—"

"Curly's?" I said. "Curly's Sea Shack? On the boardwalk?"

"I don't know any others. Yeah, he's sick of it. He wants to move to Florida and run fishing trips. That's gonna be a disaster because that man knows nothing about fishing, but not my call." He shrugged again.

I turned on David when we got outside. "You're pretty good at making stuff up, aren't you? I'd hate to be married to you, or something."

He stopped and looked at me very seriously. "I'd never lie to you, Ginger. I think one of your magical powers is that you would see right through it." He smiled, then started walking away, heading toward the Roman Villa Motel. In a short time, he seemed to have gotten to know me better than anyone. I disliked that about him.

One day we followed Yolanda to a restaurant on the boardwalk. She was having lunch with a belly dancer whose stage name was Sheba. While my parents knew several strippers with hearts of gold, they generally did not socialize with them, because they never worked at the same clubs. Belly dancers, who were still seen as a little racy at that time, were considered more socially acceptable, however. Sheba had a BA from Smith and, like other belly dancers, had spent years perfecting her craft, according to my mother. Sheba was not working at Curly's, which had a family friendly image, but at the somewhat more sophisticated Coast of Capri, a restaurant and bar a few blocks down the boardwalk.

"How do you suppose a woman looks when she's having an affair?" David asked. We were sitting at an outside table at the restaurant where Yolanda and Sheba were eating inside and there was loud samba music playing on tinny speakers.

I snorted. "You'll never know," I told him.

He rolled his eyes. "You look lovely in the moonlight," he said. It was about one in the afternoon.

"Shut up. It's not my fault we have to do this. I told my mother we'd watch her. Do you like cigarette holders?" Yolanda was sitting at a table by the window inside, gesturing with a long ebony cigarette holder. "I'd want one a lot if I wasn't worried they were kind of pretentious."

David was signaling the waiter, but stopped to look at me. "Someday, I hope you'll say that about me," he said.

"What?"

"I hope you'll say, 'I'd want him a lot if I wasn't worried he was kind of pretentious.' That would be a start." He smiled. "You know, sometimes people think the cello, it's a bit showy." He turned to the waiter. "We'll have the seafood platter and a bottle of champagne," he told him.

The waiter, a 19-year-old surfer, looked confused. "I'm not sure what we got…."

"You find out and get us some," David told him with authority. The surfer shuffled off.

"I can't pay for that, you know." I suddenly was reminded with a cold, sickening jolt that I couldn't pay for anything.

"I want to take care of it. Please."

"You really don't have to spend so much."

"When the girl says that, you know the date's going well."

"Is this a date? I don't think I've been on a date before."

David laughed. "Me neither. I know about five people my age."

"That's more than I do. My mom keeps telling me I'm having a wonderful childhood. But I think she's really the one who's having a wonderful childhood."

I looked around at the restaurant, which was nicer than I'd realized when we sat down. "You know, I've been to good restaurants before. We just don't pay. Are you going to pay?"

"Uh-huh."

"Will you have any money left?"

"I've been saving up for years to go to college to study music. You know, what kids usually do: paper route, stock boy, playing cello at weddings. Then, when I applied, I got a scholarship, a stipend and a fellowship. That's why we're going to spend the summer behaving like we're rich. Because I am, just for the time being. We can do whatever you want."

I forgot myself for a moment and got excited. "I'd like to go to a diner. We never go to diners because it's too humiliating to skip out on them."

"Slumming. Rich people go slumming at diners. We're rich now, remember. So we can go slumming. We'll dress up. When you dress elegantly and go to a diner, it shows you're just kidding."

The waiter brought a bottle of cold duck, an American champagne. "To Paris," David toasted.

"Oh. Yeah. To Paris."

"You must be good. At the cello," I said. David shrugged. "That must be nice. I used to be good at ballet, but I had to stop because the teacher tried to punch my mother. That's why I had to stop piano, too."

"Okay, don't look up," David said.

"That's the worst thing to say to a person. I have to look up now."

"Your father is coming."

My father came down the boardwalk, walking right past us in our disguises but stepping inside for a moment to say hello to Yolanda and Sheba. Then he walked next door, to the Biscayne Bay Motel, and disappeared inside a room.

"What an amateur," I almost shouted. "You can tell he's never had an affair before. Going to a motel in broad daylight. I'm so ashamed."

"Here comes Julie," David said.

She walked up the beach, then onto the boardwalk and over to the motel. She was wearing sunglasses and a floppy hat, just like us. She entered the room where my father was. After about five minutes, David went over to the motel and pushed a note under their door. With my left hand I had written, "We are watching you."

*

David and I spent a lot of time together, looking for things to do as we investigated my father's social life. One day, although it was against everything I stood for, David coaxed me onto a roller coaster called the Tsunami. I hated roller coasters. I couldn't understand why being terrified would be entertaining. Like going out for dinner at a nice restaurant and having the waiter hang you over a cliff for a while as part of the fun. Just not entertaining. But for some reason I let David talk me into it.

We got on, and the roller coaster cars moved slowly along an old-fashioned wooden track, clicking menacingly. We started heading up a steep hill, but still slowly. Then, all of a sudden, we hurtled forward and down, with the ground racing towards us at breathtaking speed. At the very last second, before we crashed into the earth, the roller coaster cars straightened out and veered to the left, making a sickening turn up another very steep hill.

We did that over and over: Your head snapping backwards as you zipped straight up, your body flying forward against the seatbelt as you careened straight down toward the concrete below. When it was over, you couldn't believe you had actually lived through it all. It was thrilling and sickening and terrifying, all at once. Your legs were shaking, but there was a certain pride in your step. It made you think: Boy, if I can survive that, I must be amazing. And yet, there was something so comforting, so right, about the solid concrete under your feet. That part made you think: Let's never do that again. Riding the Tsunami—and liking it—were definitely things you could only do in small steps.

Chapter 9

I thought that my father's affair with Julie was a secret, but I soon came to realize that every act working in Driftwood that summer was probably aware of what was going on, and also trying to keep my mother in the dark.

One day I was walking down the boardwalk with my mother, a tap dancer named Betty Wayne and her husband, a man called Roderigo. I have never seen another act like Roderigo's. He looked like an opera singer—a very big man with a pointy, waxed moustache and thick black hair. He always wore suits and walked with his chest out, as pompous as an opera star. He was introduced to the audience as an international singing celebrity, just back from a tour of Italy. He would stride onto the stage with his chin held high, a cape over his shoulders, with the band playing bold opera music. People would begin to shuffle in their seats, wondering how long this dull recital would take. Then he would throw open his arms, close his eyes and begin to sing, but his voice was as tiny and high-pitched as Mickey Mouse's. He would press through an entire aria in this itsy bitsy voice, gesturing and striding around as if he were a bullfighter with the voice of a flea.

People were stunned. In fact, Roderigo often had an extraordinary effect on audiences. Acts spoke about him in hushed tones because of one particularly memorable accomplishment. At a show where my mother had also performed, a woman in the audience laughed so hard at Roderigo's act that she peed, then fell out of her chair and knocked out her dentures. This was a fabled achievement.

Off stage, Roderigo was a nice man with a normal voice and a serious weight problem. On that day, we were just about to go into a restaurant on the boardwalk when he sharply steered my mother away from it and practically pushed her toward the beach.

"Let's not go there today, Dorothy," he said. "We go there all the time. It's boring."

"Oh, come on, Rod. I love the fried clams there. It's not any more boring than the rest of New Jersey, either." Her voice sounded husky and tired. While everyone else had a deepening tan already, my mother just seemed to get paler as the summer went on.

I noticed that Betty the tap dancer was anxiously watching the restaurant while the other two bickered. I turned around and saw my dad and Julie sitting at a table right by the window, holding hands.

"NO," my mother was saying, as Roderigo dragged her around the boardwalk, pointing at hot dog stands and coffee shops. "I want fried clams. I'll go in alone if I have to. Lord knows I spend enough of my time alone." He had her by the wrist, but she was yanking away and turning toward the restaurant.

In desperation, Roderigo suddenly threw open his arms and, in the middle of the boardwalk, started to sing a song from his act, a jazzy number called "All of Me." He started snapping his fingers and tapping his toes, just like a member of a 1950s boy band, but all the while singing like Mickey Mouse. People walking on the boardwalk stopped to watch him, some of them laughing, some of them too astonished to know what to do.

"What's wrong with you?" my mother shouted at him, trying to be heard over his amazingly loud squeaky voice. "You really need a lot of attention, don't you?" In the meantime, I saw that my father and Julie had noticed all the fuss. They quietly left the restaurant and scuttled off in different directions. Betty patted my arm as we watched them go.

"Don't worry, honey," she said. "But that was a close one."

All of the acts got one night a week off. That night, the Meterry Sisters were off. The opening act who replaced them was The Amazing Almanzo. He brought out a large gym bag that he set in the middle of the stage. It contained triangles and bowling pins that he would juggle. Then, just when you were getting a little bored with the juggling, the gym bag moved. Almanzo would jump back, alarmed, then spend some time cautiously easing up to it. When he finally looked inside, he would fall backwards as a tall elegant woman emerged, limb by limb, from the bag. She was a contortionist, someone who could fold herself into a gym bag if need be, basically. The audience never ceased to be amazed.

You had to wonder how these two found each other. Was he hanging out in ladies' gymnastics classes when he saw her and realized she could make his fortune? Was there tension in their relationship, given that his only real contribution to the powerhouse part of the act was unzipping the zipper? Did his in-laws resent him for making a living by smashing their daughter into a gym bag? Or was she the mastermind behind the act? Had they tried it the other way around and found that having a guy come out of the bag just didn't have the same pizzazz? There was undoubtedly a rich and wondrous back story to each of these acts.

My mother came on next and I stood in the dressing room, watching her through the curtain that leads to the stage. After a while I realized my father was standing behind me.

"How's my girl?" he asked. "Hmm? Pumpkin?" I ignored him. I had managed not to say more than a couple of words to him since I'd discovered his affair.

"She's good tonight, isn't she?" he said, nodding toward my mother. He waited for a few more moments of silence. "Ginger, you have to talk to me. Someday? Yes? Sweetheart?" I could hear the floor boards squeak behind me as he shifted his weight, waiting for an answer.

"Ginger, you have to understand that when you're an artist you are not like other people and—"

"Dad, you make poodles out of balloons. Don't tell me about the artistic temperament."

He laughed. "So I do. I understand that you despise me. That's good, actually. I wouldn't have it any other way. It's because you love your mother that you feel so strongly."

I snorted but kept staring at the stage.

"Don't you ever hate her, though?" my father asked finally. "Just a little? When she's taken credit for something you know was your idea alone? Or humiliated you in public for some supposedly criminal act that's just pitifully human? She does these things to you, too. I see that. Are you ever frightened of her? Does she make you feel worthless, just a little, sometimes?"

On the stage, my mother was starting into her finale, "Glowworm."

"Maybe not," he said, as we both watched. "That's good. She does me, though. So I find myself, at this advanced age, looking for… comfort elsewhere. And actually falling in love for the first time."

I noticed that he was tearing up a little. I thought about how different he had looked with Julie. But I could only feel horrified and sad. Your parents were supposed to keep their love lives to themselves. I liked it that way.

My mother had the mallets with the worm and was beginning to play.

"It's the act of a weak man, I know," my father continued, "but that's why she scares me, isn't it?" He grabbed me by the shoulders and yanked me around to face him. "I just want you to understand, Ginger."

He waited silently for a response, but I simply stared at him, not ready to be sympathetic. Finally he smiled and looked at the floor. "I

86

wanted to name you Katherine," he said. "Funny. All right, then. We've said what we have to say, right?"

"I'm ashamed of you, Dad."

He smiled sadly again. "I'm afraid you always will be."

I went down to the beach and walked straight into the water, clothes and all, wondering how far I would dare to go. I got up to my shoulders, but then I thought about all the jellyfish and the sardines swarming around me and went back to the shoreline. David usually showed up when I went to the beach, but tonight he wasn't there. I lay on the cool sand for a long time, then I walked home, partially covered in sand. It was so late that the show at Curly's was over and I could hear the DJ playing "Live and Let Die" for the late-night teenage crowd.

Our house was pitch black except for a glowing red dot on the porch—my mother's cigarette. The porch screen door squealed as I opened it.

"Where the heck have you been?" she hissed.

"Out. Somewhere." I was so tired I swayed a little and still sodden with ocean water and sand.

"I need you to come with me," she said. "I think he's at Yolanda's." She got up and started pushing me toward the sidewalk.

"No, that's ridiculous, she's not the—" I started to stammer, then thought better of it. "I mean, I know you think he's seeing Yolanda, but he's probably taking a walk. I've been following him for days, and I have never seen him with Yolanda. That's the truth. I have no reason to believe he's seeing Yolanda."

"No reason to believe? What does that mean?"

"He's not seeing her. I'm sure."

She had already pushed me a block down the street by the time I sputtered this out. She was a small but weirdly powerful woman. Before I knew it we were at Yolanda's house, a bungalow a few blocks closer to the beach that was slightly bigger and nicer than ours. My mother climbed into some bushes across the street and tugged me in after her.

"We should not be doing this," I whispered as we squatted and tried to keep branches out of our eyes. "Let's just go home. I'll follow him tomorrow, I promise."

"No, I need to know. He keeps going on walks; all night long, he's walking." She grabbed my arm, poking her nails into the skin. "I'm afraid this could be worse than I thought."

Eventually I fell asleep, resting my head in her lap. Then I felt sharp pokes in my ribs, and heard laughter across the street. There were a few lights on in Yolanda's house, and we could see a man's silhouette moving around inside.

I lay back down and looked at the sky.

"Maybe it's Reynolds," I whispered. He was Yolanda's dancing partner.

"He's gay," my mother hissed.

"So, they're socializing."

"Not at 2 in the morning."

The man was on the porch steps now. He gave Yolanda a quick kiss, then walked up the street, past the bush where we were hiding. I knew it had to be Reynolds, so I lay back in the grass and stared at the stars in the sky. The man's footsteps clicked by us. Men didn't wear sneakers all the time in those days, even at the beach, so it could have been anyone.

I looked over at my mother. She had her hand pressed hard against her chest and was breathing hard. "Are you all right?" I whispered. She shushed me and continued to stare ahead of her with crazy eyes, breathing heavily.

"I told you," she gasped finally. "You think I'm a fool. You both think I'm a fool, but I'm not."

"You just watched a man through some bushes," I told her. "You couldn't even see him clearly." I was quite certain my mother was going to see what she wanted to see at that point.

She shook her head, her crazy eyes swimming around. "I told you," she said.

I did not go to Curly's for days after that. It was fun to be childish, though, with the problems of grown-ups too much on my mind. I barely left the house and hardly spoke to either of my parents. This was not particularly unusual behavior for me, and they seemed to take little notice, both caught up in their own dramas. I may seem chatty to you, but at that time many people found me quiet enough to seem odd.

When they went out in the evenings to do their shows I would ransack the house for my mother's cigarettes and then smoke as many as I could find. This was a game we had been playing since I was around 10. Over the years she had hidden them in ingenious places: in the flour canister, the vacuum cleaner or the freezer. She definitely became trickier as time went on. We never discussed the game, and I never smoked in front of her. But we both knew about and, I think now, secretly enjoyed the challenge.

Chapter 10

Although I was trying to boycott the family drama, I finally decided to break down and go to Curly's one night. I showed up a while before the show was supposed to start. We usually ate after a show, but I was hungry early and I knew Curly would let me order whatever I wanted, so it seemed like the best idea. The bar was on a raised level at the back of the club, with several small tables running parallel to it, like a small mezzanine. I settled myself at a table at the very back of that mezzanine where the entertainers and the band usually sat because it was farthest from the stage and didn't offer a great view for paying customers.

I was eating french fries and thinking about my father. That summer made me stop and consider him more. Like many kids, I had generally thought about Dorothy and Ted as two people who had come together to be my parents. I knew they had rich, sometimes unfathomable lives beyond just our little domestic paradise, but in my mind, they existed mainly to take care of me. And if I was going to spend any time thinking about them as individuals, that time would be mainly devoted to my mother, who did know how to command your attention. Conversely, my father was defined by gentlemanly self-effacement. And that never seemed to change, on stage or off. My mother was exuberant and almost girlish on stage. Off stage, she often seemed to burst into every room yelling, then would moderate her approach based on circumstances. My father, on the other hand, was never anything but the man we saw on stage.

A woman named Edie, the band's saxophonist, who had a drinking problem that left her perpetually tipsy, came and sat with me. My father, who had been getting some ginger ale at the bar to take backstage, passed our table. He leaned over and placed a Shirley Temple with extra cherries in front of me—my favorite drink—then patted my head as he walked on.

"Such a thoughtful guy," Edie sighed, carefully resting her head on one hand as she watched him. I nodded, holding onto a cherry stem and dangling it over my mouth so I could grab the cherry with my teeth.

"And a great musician."

"He's not a musician," I said, then felt bad, because Edie was already quite tipsy and clearly confused.

"Oh, sure, honey. He's a great bassist. Or was, I should say. Hasn't played in years as far as I know."

"Okay," I said cautiously.

She nodded philosophically. "You know, sometimes it's hard to have two musicians in one family. Or two plumbers, for all I know." She laughed a little too hard. "But it didn't work out for him. To keep it up. No matter how much he loved jazz."

"Jazz?" I was beginning to wonder if I should find someone to help Edie. Usually, her sleepy and vague demeanor didn't seem to interfere with her ordinary life, but she seemed to be very confused about my father. My parents loved show tunes. We had cast albums to "The Sound of Music," "My Fair Lady," even "Cabaret," which my mother thought was somewhat vulgar but had some great numbers. Once my parents had waltzed around the living room to "Shall We Dance" from "The King and I," then my dad had picked me up in his arms and danced with me, too. They didn't seem to like anything else. "Turn that off!" my mother would shout at the TV, even if it was only showing an upbeat Tony Bennett song. It didn't seem like a household where anybody loved jazz.

Edie was reminiscing some more. "He was even in a band back in…." She narrowed her eyes, peering in her mind across the farmland and plains to find the name of his hometown.

"Sheboygan," she pronounced.

"Cleveland," I said, unable to hide my annoyance at her confusion.

"Cleveland," she agreed decisively.

"Now if I was him, I'd keep my mouth shut, too. Learn to let some things slide."

My sympathy for her was growing thin. "Because jazz is scary, or something?"

She shook her head. "No," she chuckled, "because that Dorothy's a barracuda." Remembering who I was, she slapped her hand across her mouth and smiled apologetically.

"Dorothy tried to do her act at some of the places he played," she finally explained. "I'd have to say the crowds were not enthusiastic." She veered sideways to look in my eyes. "You know, jazz people like to think they're better than some of that corny stuff she plays." She sat up and pulled herself together. "But one night, they were playing in this place in Newark? Very cool, you know? And, I think people started laughing. I think it was bad. Dorothy didn't want anything to do with it again. She didn't want Ted being involved either. Done." She chopped her hand down on the table. She sighed. "He let it slide for her, I think, which was nice. I can't blame the guy, because she's kind of a dragon. I mean, you could understand why he would—" She widened her eyes abruptly and looked at me.

"Ginger!" she said, as if suddenly remembering again who I was. "You are so grown up now, Ginger. What are you in—college? And so beautiful." She stuck her head in her purse, pulling out some cigarettes. "Gotta go set up, sweetie. Nice talking to you."

After she left, I noticed a hubbub around the large semicircular booth facing the stage at the front of the mezzanine, arguably the best seat in the house. Looking closer, I realized that Larry was there and he was attracting a steady stream of fans. The show hadn't started yet, and Larry was trying to gracefully deflect the attention he was receiving, but it was clear that everyone in the room was aware of him. Curly was sitting on his left and Herbie on his right.

It was a Thursday, in some ways the start of the weekend, but still typically a slow night. My mother was opening, followed by Reynolds and Yolanda, then my father. My mother usually had a certain hauteur about her, as if she had learned the xylophone from her father, a European archduke. Tonight, clearly aware of Larry's arrival, she came out with a desperate smile on her face, shoving the xylophone so hard in front of her that she lost control of it and it almost flew off the front of the stage. She chased after it and caught it just before it careened into the audience, laughing a little hysterically as she centered it properly on the stage. No one seemed too perturbed about her behavior, though, since Larry's presence had leant a sort of party atmosphere to the club, so much so that there seemed to be little interest in watching the acts. She launched into "Flight of the Bumblebee," playing it even faster than usual and looking up occasionally with an insane grin on her face. She finished to a smattering of applause and the roar of people carrying on their own hilarious conversations. Her playing got quieter with each number, until the band nearly drowned out "Glowworm." The audience did pull itself together to applaud as she took her last bow, and Larry yelled "Bravo" as she backed robotically off the stage, her face a peculiar mixture of terror and rage.

Someone had spotted me just as my mother was coming on, so I had moved to Larry's table at his insistence by the time my mother emerged to sit with him after her act.

"Was I good?" she asked anxiously.

"You were fantastic, Duchess," Larry said. "Never better."

Herbie, a guy who had been teaching himself since childhood the best ways to take the wind out of someone's sails, looked up from his shrimp cocktail. "Nice set, honey," he said. My mother gave him a savage look, recognizing pity when she heard it.

Unfortunately, Reynolds and Yolanda were on next and had managed to capture the crowd's attention. They had quieted down and were watching with far greater interest than they had shown earlier.

"These two are great!" Larry said. My mother was shredding paper napkins into a large pile in front of her.

My father also killed. One woman went into an uncontrollable giggling fit after he put a balloon Easter hat on her head and tried to get her to play "Mary Had a Little Lamb" on a kazoo. The ridiculousness of his act was always a little funnier because of my father's English accent and debonair manner. She was so overcome with hysteria that the woman's husband eventually had to lead her from the stage and settle her down back in her seat, which any performer would consider a great success. We could hear little shrieks of occasional laughter from her for quite a while.

As Larry laughed along with the crowd, my mother reached for his hand. "We're still on, right?"

"Of course, Duchess. The wheels are turning."

At that moment Reynolds and Yolanda walked by, in their street clothes and on their way home.

"Hello!" said the insistently outgoing Larry. "I loved your act! Won't you sit with us?"

My mother took a long slug of her Bacardi cocktail, chomping energetically on some ice cubes as everyone else shifted over to let Reynolds and Yolanda join us.

"It's such an honor to have you here, Mr. Davenport!" Reynolds said. He was blond and boyish, and he leaned toward Larry adoringly.

"My pleasure to see such great acts tonight, including you and your lovely lady."

95

"You're so kind," Yolanda said, inclining her head and smiling.

Throughout their conversation my mother would shout out "Ha!" at random moments while still gnawing on her ice cubes. Then the worst happened: Someone noticed that Julie was sitting at the bar, even though the Meterry Sisters were off that night. She was wearing white bell bottoms and a poncho she had clearly crocheted herself. When I saw that she was also wearing sunglasses in the darkened night club, I knew that she must be there to meet my father after his show, since she was dumb enough to believe her outfit would serve as a disguise.

Of course the growing crowd at our table insisted that she join us. She put her hand to her mouth when Curly called to her, looking around furtively as if she was hoping to sneak away. Finally, she slid off her stool reluctantly and came over.

"Hi, everyone," she said. "I was just here having a Coke." She waved her drink around to prove it, sloshing some on Reynolds. Her darting eyes finally settled on Larry and she stopped dead.

"Oh, I didn't know Mr. Davenport was here." She shook her head hard. "Really, I had no idea."

"I'm Larry, honey, nice to meet you. Please join us." Larry was pointing to a wedge of seat that was still left at the end of the booth as everyone tried to squish closer together.

"My sisters would die if they knew I was meeting him alone," Julie breathed to Hector, a waiter on his break who she ended up sitting next to at the edge of the booth.

"Hey, who let this scoundrel in?" My father, fresh from finishing his act, pulled up a chair to the crammed booth and straddled it backwards. He and Larry shook hands across the table. Julie had her right hand resting along the side of her face, seemingly to prevent her from seeing my father, because if she looked at him I guess that would somehow make it clear that they were involved. I sometimes had to suppress an urge to take her aside and teach her how to conduct an affair. My mother, meantime, was watching Yolanda and silently mimicking her exuberant facial expressions, perhaps without even realizing it. Every once in a while Larry would see her and ask, "Are you feeling okay, Dot?"

"That was the best balloon act I've seen today, my friend." Larry told my father solemnly.

My father smiled happily. "Yes, and I always say I have never heard anything like your singing."

"Well, I'm glad you said that, my friend, because I was going to invite you and your gang up to see my show when you have a night off."

"Wow!" Reynolds said.

"Fantastic!" Curly said.

My mother gasped in horror. "I think he just meant Ted and—" she started, looking appalled, but she was drowned out by the group's excitement.

"My sisters," Julie rasped, reaching her hands out in an appeal, "they would just die if—"

"Then prop 'em up and bring 'em along," Herbie said. Hector the waiter had left, so Herbie was now sitting next to Julie. He gave her a hearty slap on the back, which knocked her off her small wedge of seat onto the floor.

"That's settled then." Larry rubbed his hands together. "Let's have another round for everyone."

Chapter 11

They set a date for the trip to see Larry, but life settled back into its routine in the meantime. I was sitting on our porch one night while my parents were at Curly's, working my way through my first pack, when David walked up, wearing a tuxedo. It was a rather shabby tuxedo. It looked like it might have come from the local thrift shop, Krupa's Krazy Klothes. But he pulled it off somehow, making it look elegant. He carried a bag in his hand.

"What do you want?" I asked. I had found a bottle of sherry hidden under the bathroom sink, so I was feeling a little hazy.

"Open the bag," he said. It contained a simple, slightly dilapidated but still beautiful black evening dress. "We're going slumming," he said.

I put on the dress and he steered me down several blocks to the most lavish diner in Driftwood, the Excelsior. It was all chrome and bright blue neon. I loved it, but had never been inside.

I don't know how he got me there. The sherry must have made me docile. I kept telling him I didn't want his dress and I wasn't hungry and he kept telling me to shut up. After a while, I thought that was very funny, but then I changed my mind and started sniffling just as we got to the diner. I was a mess in those days, apparently. The diner was full of middle-of-the-night customers, truck drivers and sleepy travelers. There were red booths and multicolored modern chandeliers that looked like someone had thrown a pack of pick-up sticks and it had frozen in mid-air.

David ordered corned beef hash for me and started asking stupid questions. What was the most humiliating thing that ever happened to me in gym? Who was the most obnoxious person I knew? Who was my favorite author? When I told him it was Dickens, he wanted to know which books I had read. I had made my way through the list and was explaining that my favorite was *Great Expectations*, because of Miss Havisham, stubborn in the face of defeat, when I looked up and saw him smiling at me, the happiest, loveliest smile.

"You are a very wonderful person, Ginger," he said.

I snorted and forked up a large mouthful of corned beef hash, getting most of it into my mouth.

"Which doesn't mean it's always easy to like you," he added.

I could tell he was still staring and smiling even though I had gone back to studiously eating my corned beef. "Ginger, you're just a beautiful girl," he finally said.

I decided not to respond, holding out to see what would come next.

"I want you to be my friend forever," he said, quietly but with great conviction. "I'm in love with you. I brought you here to this diner tonight to tell you that. Do you understand? I wanted it to be special. Because you said you liked diners."

I shook my fork, corned beef hash flying off of it. "You're not in love with me," I said.

"Don't tell me that," he said, his voice husky with anger. "No matter how smart we are, there are a lot of things in the world we know nothing about. What about all the things in the world that you don't know? Like how I feel about you. If you're not as smart as you think you are, you could be missing a lot."

I hated that idea—that there was an infinite number of things I could be missing every second of every day because of the limits of my own little world.

David would not shut up. "I love how you scare anyone who comes within 20 feet of you. And yet you ran three blocks down the boardwalk after that family whose kid dropped a stuffed bear out of his stroller because you were worried the kid would have been heartbroken without it."

"Then the family started screaming when I caught up to them."

I watched him struggle not to laugh at the memory—of the nice family reacting in terror to the demonic girl dressed in black running after them, shouting at them to stop. Then he recovered himself. "Philistines," he said.

"I love how you spit in the eye of practically everyone you meet," he continued, "but you're terrified of the spinning teacups at the amusement pier."

"So many people throw up on those teacups every day."

Then I stopped and realized the real problem. "I'm not going to sleep with you, or anything, you know," I told him. The corned beef hash had sobered me up a bit, but I was still slurring my words.

"I don't care. Because I believe one day we're going to live in Paris. No matter how stubborn you are I will make that happen one day. I want you to keep that in mind."

"Oh yeah, we'll live on stipends and passion for our art, huh? I don't think that's going to work." I squinted to try to get him in focus. "You're a really nice guy, David, don't get me wrong. But what people mostly don't understand about me is, I just want to be left alone. Get a nine-to-five job, retire at 65, die in my bed, contented. I don't want anybody to mess with that dream."

He picked up my hand and pulled it gently toward him. As I watched, too tired to react, he kissed each of my fingers. Then he leaned over and said, with great confidence, "You're bluffing."

Chapter 12

A week later, on a Thursday night, a small caravan made the trip down the Garden State Parkway to see Larry's show in Atlantic City. Everyone who had been at Larry's table at Curly's that night, including Curly, had conspired to get the night off on an evening when Larry was working. Larry, who was apparently pathologically nice, sent two limos. They were old-school limos, not stretch but extra long black cars with enough room for about five or six passengers. In our car, my parents and Curly sat on the roomy back seat, with Reynolds and Yolanda on two jump seats that faced them and me in front with the driver, a guy named Esteban. In the other car were the Meterry Sisters and David, plus Roderigo and Betty.

Before gambling, Atlantic City was not the home of flashing slot machines, high rollers and glitzy decoration that it would become. In fact, it was a sleepy and slightly seedy waterfront resort that attracted only a fraction of the vacationers who might have once come there. It had been a popular resort early in the century, and it still had beautiful old hotels that rambled along the beach in their 1920s splendor. There were enormous sitting rooms with windows overlooking the beach, furnished with fading chintz sofas and long-abandoned grand pianos. When my parents played there, usually at some lounge a couple of blocks from the beach, I would sneak off and sit in one of those rooms, looking at the water and imagining that life could still be so elegant.

When our limos pulled up to the hotel where Larry was performing, no doorman rushed to open the door and there was little other fanfare. Instead, a few surprised Philadelphians on holiday stood around watching to see who emerged. They seemed pleased with what they saw. My mother and Yolanda were both dressed for a night out, each in their signature styles. My mother was wearing the same long gold dress that she'd been wearing when we found her in the phone booth. It was her most impressive performance outfit. Her hair was piled on her head and trails of black liner slithered around her eyes like snakes. Yolanda was in a shorter red dress with a plunging neckline. She wore her thick black hair in a high ponytail, but her assertive makeup was similar to my mother's. Both Reynolds, who must have had a first name, and my father were dapper in black suits. David and I followed them, wearing the fancy outfits we'd worn to the diner. Roderigo sported the black cape with the red lining that he wore in his act and Betty, who was going through a spiritual phase, wore a shimmering blue sari. Curly wore his own customary uniform—forest green Bermuda shorts and a brightly colored Hawaiian shirt, along with black leather sandals and white socks. The Meterry Sisters glittered in pastel rhinestones, their hair towering like skyscrapers. Our entrance was a bit like the opening to a movie directed by an intern that Fellini had fired.

The people at the hotel—who had previously been standing around looking at the ocean and wondering what to do with themselves—actually broke out into timid and confused applause. My mother and Roderigo both stopped and bowed deeply, but everyone else swept by the bewildered tourists.

Inside—at the Beachcomber Lounge—Herbie, who opened for Larry, was moving toward the end of his act. We caused a bit of a commotion as we burst into the room. There were at most 75 people there—and that was a huge crowd for a Thursday night in Atlantic City at that time, all brought in by Larry's fame—so our group of about a dozen was certainly noticed as we made our noisy way to our tables.

"Oh, look," Herbie said, as our entrance interrupted his act, "bingo at Bellevue just let out." He narrowed his eyes at us, peeved at the disruption, then went on with his routine.

Next Larry came on, opening with "Moondance," which had been a hit for Van Morrison a couple of years earlier. My mother sat back in her chair and watched him with a crooked, self-satisfied smile on her face. At the next table, the Meterry Sisters giggled uncontrollably. When the song ended, he lit a cigarette and did some audience patter, talking about how happy he was to be in Atlantic City, what a great crowd they were and so forth.

"And I want to extend a special welcome to some show biz friends who I see are here tonight." He ran quickly through everyone's name, even David and me. The Meterry Sisters giggled even louder and Roderigo and my father waved exuberantly, shouting "Bravo." Then Larry launched into his next song, finally winding up after a few numbers with "The Summer Wind."

I don't know how it happened, but David and I somehow ended up in a limo with his sisters and my dad. I thought my mother was in the other limo, which had left before ours, but she wasn't home when we got there. Or when I got there, since my father insisted on getting out with the Meterrys "to make sure they got into their house all right." The house was right there, you could see it from the limo, a cute little Cape Cod, safe and sound and waiting for them on a quiet Thursday in Driftwood. David sighed and smiled at me as he followed them out of the car. I watched as my father and Julie peeled off and walked toward the beach and David and the other two sisters went into the house. The limo drove several blocks farther from the ocean, then sailed up silently in front of our empty house. I sat smoking in our screened in porch, reading a book called *The Primal Scream*, about how you could solve your problems by yelling your head off.

My father came home first, about 45 minutes later. "It's late, Kitten. You should get to bed," he said, kissing my head and walking past me to the bedroom. My mother arrived a couple of hours later, around 2, chauffeured in what must have been yet another limousine. The chauffeur got out and opened her door, which I thought was particularly elegant, until I saw that my mother was so rubbery-legged and drunk that she needed help walking from the curb. I opened the screen door and stepped out and he transferred her weight to me and slipped away.

"Chincher!" she declared loudly, staring at me with the exaggerated interest of the truly inebriated, chewing the syllables of my name like they were chunks of bread. I dumped her on the wicker love seat and watched her struggle to sit up properly. Drunks are a little bit like toddlers in the way they pull themselves up from falling on their faces so cheerfully.

"Chincher! Hazen this been a magical night?" She stared attentively at the lamp next to the love seat, and I wondered if she thought it was me.

"A magical night," she continued. She surprised me by turning her head abruptly to look at me. "Did you know I'm going to Hollywood?"

"To be on 'Dean Martin'?" I asked.

She tried to slap her hand down on the love seat's arm, missed, and had to recover from almost falling forward. "Jush the beginning, Chincher. Jush the beginning." She nodded her head a few times, then her chin dropped onto her chest and in a moment I could hear light snoring. I got up then and pulled her sideways so that she could stretch out on the love seat. I put down the book and went to bed.

Chapter 13

And then the rains came.

They began in mid-July, day after day of unrelenting rain. Rain poured down in torrents on the beach and the boardwalk, on the roller coasters and the miniature golf courses. It washed away children's chalk drawings on the sidewalks in front of bungalows and nearly swept the lifeguard boats out to sea. It brought about the cancellation of the boardwalk buggy parade and kids' beauty pageant, and hundreds of vacationers' plans.

Inside stores, harried parents desperately tried to prevent bored children from destroying the merchandise. Couples sat in restaurants, seeing each other's flaws more clearly in the grey light. Surfers and volleyball players huddled in the dry spots under the boardwalk, hoping for a break in the weather and watching their tans fade.

After a couple of weeks of regularly returning rain, people gave up. In motels up and down the beach, tourists raced about their rooms, stuffing their belongings into suitcases and then tossing their bags and kids into the car. For days, a stream of cars lined the road out of Driftwood marked, "To Garden State Parkway." People rescheduled their vacations, making last minute reservations in other resorts that were popular at the time, like the Poconos or the Catskills, instead of the Jersey shore.

David and I would go to the piers that had the amusement rides. A few people kept their rides open, so we would ride the Ferris Wheel, holding an umbrella but drenched, or sit inside a little car in a train that snaked all the way around the pier. I can remember laughing so hard, although I don't remember what the jokes were. But so hard.

Sometime during the second week of rain, I sat in a coffee shop with my parents, who were having breakfast with a harmonica player named Mel. Mel had very large lips, and I always wondered if he got them from playing or if you had to have big lips to play the harmonica. He also spoke like a harmonica, with his voice rising and falling up and down through each sentence, as if he were running his mouth back and forth on the harmonica.

"Good day for ducks," he said, as we stared out at the rain. I don't think he meant to talk that way. Just too much time alone with a harmonica.

The Meterry Sisters and David were in another booth at the far end of the restaurant. As usual, the women's conversation was punctuated with giggles and whoops, while David watched them with affectionate amusement. Curly entered the shop, and looked around. It was pretty full, given the lack of much else to do. He came nervously up to our table and sat down. He had been using a newspaper as an umbrella and black newsprint ran down the sides of his face.

"Unbelievable, huh?" he said, wiping his face and signaling the waitress for coffee. "Two weeks of rain. I think it's a record."

He slurped some coffee when it came, then looked anxiously at my mother. "I got another cancellation, Dottie," he said. As was usually the case, we all accepted the idea that if someone was going to talk about business, they would be addressing my mother. "The Arlington Police Benevolent Association will not be spending their vacation in Driftwood. I mean, Noah's Ark by the Sea. So, a midweek banquet—gone. All that revenue—gone. It sucks, I'm telling you."

My mother was smoking and watching Curly suspiciously. My father was trying to catch glimpses of Julie's reflection in a mirror behind my mother.

"Curly, you can't cancel us for the rest of the summer," my mother said. "We have a contract."

"Yeah, yeah, I know that, Dorothy. I'm just thinking I don't know about next year. It could be we're kaput."

My mother put out her cigarette in her coffee saucer with slow, dangerous strokes. She may have believed she was on the verge of stardom, but being cancelled at Curly's was too much humiliation. She also just loved a fight.

"So, how are you going to get people to come to the club if you don't have acts?" she sneered.

Curly smiled happily. "I'm thinking this rock-and-roll thing might be all I need. Costs me almost nothing to have a DJ, and the kids love it."

"I don't know anything about that. That's because I'm an adult. That's who's got the money—adults. That's who you've got to cater to."

"Yeah, I know, Dottie. But I'm not getting a lot of money as it is, see? What have adults done for me lately? That's what I'm asking."

My mother tilted her head to the side and narrowed her eyes. "Eight years we've been coming to this deadbeat town. People love us, don't they, Ted?"

"Sure," my father said, his eyes squinting at the mirror.

"We've had other offers, Curly," my mother continued, "but we've stuck with you. That won't happen any longer." She smiled knowingly. "No, that won't happen any longer." She turned to my father. "I know what you want, you want to go on cruise ships." My parents knew many performers who were booked to entertain on cruise ships, doing shows each night as the ship sailed from port to port in the Caribbean. Cruise ships were considered a sort of easy retirement for acts who had grown tired of traveling from town to town, or who weren't getting booked any more. At that time, most cruise travelers were retirees, and they remained enthusiastic about a lot of performers whose acts were no longer popular in clubs.

"You think it's all tropical fun and games," she continued, leaning toward my father dangerously. "Well, it's not. Do you know what kinds of acts go on cruise ships, Ted? Acts that are dead, that's who. And we're not dead yet." Curly looked down and stirred his coffee nervously. My father turned and focused his full attention on my mother.

"Dorothy, it's over," he said. "Face it."

At night, if the rain stopped for a while, I would go to the beach with David and he would teach me how to dance. He taught me the cha cha and the hora and the tango. I don't know what those people did at nights in Louisiana, but now I was ready for anything. I don't think I ever got one right, but I wasn't trying to impress him. And he didn't seem to care.

"When we live in Paris, Ginger, we'll do this sort of thing all the time," he told me one night. "Dance in the rain, canoe down the Seine, eat breakfast on the Pont Neuf at dawn."

"All right," I told him. I was so tired by then, and it seemed silly to disagree.

"Yes? You said you believe that?"

"I said all right."

He leaned back on one of the posts under the boardwalk as the rain started again. We had been spending a lot of time under the boardwalk, listening to the sound of people shuffling by overhead and hunting for lost jewelry or quarters.

"When I imagine Paris, Ginger, I'm afraid I don't picture telephone poles, though. You may not be able to live out your dream of becoming a telephone lineman."

"That's okay," I told him, "there are a lot of ordinary things to do in Paris. People underestimate the French."

Eventually the sun came out. The boardwalk was once again filled with the smell of cotton candy and roasted nuts, and the sound of screaming rang from the amusement piers as children hurtled around on rickety rides. But it was not quite the same as it had been. A lot of people had already cancelled their summer beach plans and come up with other ideas. The crowds were smaller and somewhat disheartened, as if they didn't really believe the beach would ever be fun again.

I took a long walk on the boardwalk on the first sunny day. I was wearing all black as always, and I probably looked paler than usual in the bright light.

As I walked by some food stands, I saw a group of about five teenage boys, a little older than me, sitting on the railing by the beach. They were very blond and healthy looking, all dressed in cutoffs and tight T-shirts. They were the kind of people who were waiting to grow up so Bruce Springsteen could write songs about their miserable adulthoods, but that day they were just looking for a new way to pass the time.

I didn't even notice them at first. Then I heard someone humming the theme song to the TV show "The Twilight Zone," and one of the boys yelled, "Hey, Morticia!"

I walked by them, staring ahead of me. I was not your typical kid and I was used to this kind of teasing. Although I never got over hating it. As I walked on, the group burst into laughter and started to follow me. One of them started to sing the theme song from "The Addams Family."

One of them grabbed my arm. "Hey, Vampirella!" I pulled away and kept walking. No one on the boardwalk seemed to notice what was happening, and I wondered what I would do if they all started grabbing me.

"You vant to suck my blood?" one asked in his best Count Dracula voice. They burst into gulping laughter and began to surround me. "Come on, suck my blood!" I dropped my head and tried to shove them away with my elbows as they grabbed at me.

"Hey Jethro! Hey Clem! Hey Half-wit Nelson!" Suddenly we all heard a loud, angry, commanding voice and it brought them to a halt. "Get away from her! Get the heck away from her NOW." It was my mother, wearing full stage makeup and a kerchief over the curlers in her hair. Together, she and I, we couldn't have been weirder looking.

She caught up to us and pushed the boys away from me. They danced backwards, laughing, but they moved off. My mother took my hand and tugged me forward.

"Aw, saved by your Mommy," one of them called.

My mother stopped and turned, very slowly. She walked up to them and shouted, "Sometimes, there are just such awful things in the world that you just need a Mommy. You," she began poking the chest of one boy until he almost fell backwards, "are an awful thing, Schmendrick."

She strode back to me and pulled me away. "Don't worry about them, baby," she said. "If they're lucky, in 10 years they'll be unemployed parking lot attendants."

I had been happy that the rain had ended, but now I longed for the safety of my tiny bedroom back at the bungalow. "I wish my life were anything but what it is," I said.

My mother sighed. "Ginger, to be truthful, a lot of your problems are self-inflicted. I mean, you weren't born dressed like you were going to a funeral at a mime convention. Nobody makes you do that."

"I'm talking about everything. Nobody else's mother plays the xylophone for a living. And nobody's father does what Dad does. I tell people he's in plastics."

She steered me toward a bench. "I want to tell you two important

112

things. First, don't ever tell your father that. It would destroy him. Second, I'm proud of you for lying about what he does. Balloon acts are a dying breed. Have been for years, he just won't admit it. And as for you, you happen to be having a very magical childhood. You know, before I got into show business, I never fit in either, but now I do. When you're different—better than other people, really—you don't run from it. You just have to find the place where you're going to shine. It's like my worm. Ordinarily, it doesn't look like much, just a piece of felt. But you switch on the blacklight, it's something special."

"So, I'm like a worm?"

She smacked me on the arm. "Come on," she said. "We'll fix you."

She took me back to the women's dressing room at Curly's. I had loved dressing rooms since I was a little girl. First, there was the fact that not everyone was allowed inside, just the show people and me. Then there was the familiar powdery perfumed smell of the makeup being used and the sound of women's voices talking and laughing as they made themselves beautiful.

My mother sat me in front of the mirror, which ran the length of one wall, with a counter and chairs in front of it. She wiped off the stark black and white makeup I wore and began rummaging in the Meterry Sisters' makeup. I didn't even bother to object. I knew they would not mind; they might even see it as a sign of friendship and bonding that we had dipped into their makeup without even asking, just like real girlfriends. And my mother wouldn't care if I objected anyway, because she did tend to live by her own rules.

She replaced my makeup with warmer, peachier colors on my eyes and cheeks and lips. She took one of Joni Meterry's ash blond wigs and pulled it over my hair.

I looked softer, certainly, and more mature. Like an anchorwoman on a TV news show or the young principal of a fancy private school. We stared at my reflection for a while. Then we couldn't help breaking into hysterical giggles, collapsing onto one another.

"Oh my God, you look like my Aunt Fanny's psychotic cousin Darlene," my mother said, tears running down her face as she laughed. "You look like you walked through a wind tunnel and got your personality sucked out of you." She took my chin in her long fingers. "Don't ever change," she sputtered through her laughter. "You're better the way you are."

When we were done in the dressing room and I had gone back to my normal hair and makeup, we went out quietly into the near-empty nightclub, where the Meterry Sisters had recently arrived and were rehearsing a new song. We got Cokes at the bar and sat down at a booth in back to watch them. They were singing a Supremes song, "Stop in the Name of Love."

They had choreographed some simultaneous dance moves, like raising their hands like a traffic cop when they shouted "Stop!" and shaking their fingers at the audience when they sang "Think it o-over." All the while, they swiveled their hips and wiggled their bottoms as if their ankles were tied together.

"You know what you're watching?" my mother asked. "We're watching the death of show business here."

I didn't know what to say, so I snorted.

"No, I'm serious. Once upon a time, this business was made up of professionals. People studied their crafts for years. Melanie, that idiot who plays the glasses? She went to the Juilliard School of Music in New York. Studied violin. Don't snort; she told me. In the city, once upon a time, they had great lounges, great places to perform at all the hotels. Even the men there looked glamorous, that's how ritzy those rooms were. I told you I once played a wedding at the Plaza Hotel, right? Those were the days. The resorts all had elegant shows. Today, what? You're in glee club one day, the next day you're in show business. And what's show business? Curly's Sea Shack."

The sisters had finished rehearsing and were talking excitedly with the band.

"But despite all that," my mother continued, "you know where my best audience was?"

I rolled my eyes and recited an answer I had heard many times. "The Shriners convention in Worcester, Mass., 1962."

"No, honey, I'm not talking about that nonsense. My best audience, the one that hung on my every move? It was you. When you were little, kid, I was the cream in your milk. Even today, no matter how much of a jerk you act like, you're still crazy about me. That's how stupid people are. I work so hard in this business I'm getting palpitations. And the whole time, the one who loved who me the most was little Morticia here." She tugged me toward her and gave me a loud kiss on the head.

"Mom, I think you're on drugs," I said, as she pulled me toward her and smashed my face into her shoulder.

"Yes, dear, I know."

We were back in the dressing room, getting ready to go home, when I noticed a shadow in the mirror behind us.

"The Mildred," I whispered.

My mother snapped her head around. It was the little dark lady with money who kept coming to our doors.

"What are you doing here?" my mother asked her.

"Dorothy, I've been trying to get in touch with you. I'm very unhappy I had to track you down," the lady, Lorraine I now remembered, said. They stared at each other a while.

"Dad's dead," Lorraine said finally.

"Dad?" I said. "Whose dad?"

"No, shut up," my mother told me. "I was sorry to hear that, of course," she told Lorraine, polite now but clearly not really meaning it. "I did receive your letter."

"You've missed the funeral, of course," Lorraine said. "But there will be a remembrance, in September, at the beach house. In Muskoka."

"Who's dead? Where's Muskoka?" I asked.

"Not too far north of Toronto," Lorraine said, apparently thinking that I was a part of the conversation.

"You're Canadian? You said the Midwest," I said.

"It's the same thing. But shut up," my mother said.

"We were hoping you could come," Lorraine said. "I'm – I'm sure he would have been happy to have you there."

My mother smiled. "Lorraine, you know his feelings about seeing me would have been mixed. Which is fine."

"But still. We'd be happy to see you there."

"Who is this woman?" I asked.

"Shut up," my mother said.

"You have a family? With a beach house?"

"Shut up," my mother said. "It's a cottage. Two bedrooms. And a sleeping loft." She turned to Lorraine. "Did he...?"

"No, Dorothy. He told me that you agreed a long time ago that you could borrow against your portion of the estate while he was alive. That's all gone now. Your portion."

"What estate?" I asked.

116

"Not even Mother's —"

"Also gone. And then some, if I understand correctly. You know all this, Dorothy."

"Did you come all this way to tell me I've squandered it all? Surely even you have better things to do."

Lorraine sighed. Out came the little pad and gold pen. "This is the date of the memorial service. This is my number. We'd love to have you there. I think it's important for family to stand together, even at this late stage in the game."

She waited a moment, staring at the floor, and I had the sense my mother was holding her breath. "We found out from his papers that you had taken a loan against the house." There was a silence, as if the women were waiting each other out.

"It wasn't a loan." You could barely hear my mother's voice.

"You signed a note, Dorothy. They weren't rich, Dorothy. They had a little, but they weren't rich. Neither are we."

My mother snorted. "Better off than me."

"Be that as it may, Jessie and Bill and I inherit the house, with your loan against it. We can't afford to hold on to it, so when we sell it we'll need to repay your portion of the loan. We can give you some time to pay us back for the loan, but you are going to have to pay it back."

Another silence. Finally my mother raised her head and looked into the mirror. She shook her head and her eyes seemed to be gazing into the middle distance. She was clearly dismissing the entire conversation.

Lorraine gave a swift nod. "As long as we understand each other. Goodbye, Dorothy, Ginger."

I watched her disentangle the dressing room curtain and walk through it. "Who was that?"

"That was my sister Lorraine."

"Your sister? You're an only child."

"If only." She sighed.

"Why didn't you tell me you had a sister?"

"I have another one. And a brother named Bill. He's a factory manager, based on the vomitous letters he sends at Christmas. Lorraine's husband, Wilf, is an anonymous cog in a company that makes something. I hated it there. Hated them, really. I never belonged there and they were happy to see me go." Something had shifted, and I had the sense that she was talking to me as a real person, not just as a parent.

"But a whole family –"

"Sometimes you have to leave some things behind."

She smiled at me philosophically, suddenly a Canadian rebel whom I'd never met before. It occurred to me that there must be a long road that takes you from a lake house in Muskoka to becoming a xylophone player who didn't pay her bills. And all because she needed to go looking for the right light for her. Once again I was reminded of how much you could miss, even much of what was all around you, in plain sight.

"What about the loan?" I knew that we skipped out on hotels and restaurants and cut a lot of corners, but this little hurdle seemed even more serious. And why had she needed the loan? Was it true that we couldn't pay our own expenses even though we skipped out on half of them?

She raised her chin and her face curled into a satisfied smile. "Nothing to worry about, Ginger. We're going to be rich soon."

Chapter 14

David and I loved the Ferris Wheel. We went on it over and over again while the shows were going on at Curly's. Some nights, they wouldn't even bother to take our tickets after a while. Once our car got to the top, we would spot the lights of ships at sea and David would make up stories about them. One was a tuna boat heading for Key West from Yazoo, Maine. People loved tuna in Yazoo, so they had a whole fleet of tuna boats, he said. Another was a cargo ship, full of cinnamon and vanilla from Madagascar. If we closed our eyes and inhaled, we could almost believe we smelled those spices. A third was a Chinese junk from Singapore that had gone way, way, way off course.

Of course, I was terrified the whole time, hanging a hundred feet in the air in a flimsy metal cage. Sounds foolhardy, no? But I didn't say anything. I just decided not to be that person, like he had suggested the time we went swimming. It didn't really work; I was that terrified girl and there was no way around it. But I learned that you could hold off the terror, if only for a little while. It could get you into some interesting situations.

Dangling in space high above the murky water, we had come to a decision: My father was only allowed to have one affair at a time, even if one of them wasn't actually real. Of course, I didn't believe he was having anything to do with Yolanda. My mother insisted he had been the man we saw that night, but she often got ideas in her head that were hard to shake. Also, I thought he really cared for Julie, so it would be particularly sleazy to fool around with Yolanda at the same time. In any case, following my father, Julie and Yolanda was becoming too much for us. We decided I would go to Yolanda and pretend I thought she was having an affair with my father. Then she would be so upset and embarrassed that she would tell my mother that there was definitely no affair happening. We sat in the Ferris Wheel car, practicing what we would say. Like:

"Yolanda, you're a lovely woman, but it's not fair to go out with someone's dad."

"Yolanda, this nonsense has gone far enough!"

"Yolanda, we think you could do better than a guy with a balloon act. How about Eddie, the Friday night ventriloquist?"

We walked up to her house late one night after the show was over. David stood on the top porch step and knocked forcefully. Yolanda opened the door, wearing a short, tight silk robe and high heels. David's jaw dropped at the sight of her and I knew I would have to take over.

"Oh, baby," Yolanda cooed in her Spanish accent. "Come in. And Mr. David, too."

It seemed suddenly as if this was something I should do alone. "David, would you wait outside?" He nodded mutely, his mouth still trying to form words, and sat down heavily on the porch steps.

She brought me into the living room of her bungalow. It was dazzling. All the usual tattered rental house furniture was covered in huge silk scarves with bright patterns. I sat awkwardly on the edge of a couch.

"You like something to drink?" she asked, smiling. I shook my head silently. "Okay, how can I help you, baby?"

"I have to ask you sort of an embarrassing question." This was not one of the lines we had practiced, but now that we were here, she was so warm and so beautiful, the house so lovely and inviting, that I had forgotten what we meant to say.

"Are you having an affair with my father?" I blurted out. Yolanda's eyebrows shot up. She rose from her chair and moved over to the couch. She sat down next to me and took my hands.

"It gives you a lot of pain, what he does, huh?" Her question came as such a surprise I had to struggle not to cry. As was the case in so many places, there was a haze of cigarette smoke in the room. I tried to focus on Yolanda sitting across from me, but the smog in the room kept wafting between us, blurring my vision.

"When I was a little girl," she was saying, "my father did this, too. I got very angry and I grew up to be someone who was not always a very friendly person. I hope this doesn't happen to you. I have been feeling so bad for you all summer. Even for your Mama, who I have to tell you is a class-A bitch. But still, she doesn't deserve what she got."

"I don't know what to do," I told her. I had meant to tell *her* what to do, but my resolve had melted away.

"I know, honey. But baby, I tell you very honestly, there is nothing going on between us. Your dad and me. We are friends. What was going on in Trenton, last spring? It's over over over."

"Over?" I repeated stupidly. This was a twist I had not expected: My mother had again gotten something right. She had actually been right about the two of them in Trenton. I had always thought I had known the worst about my parents—it all seemed so obvious—and yet now it seemed I had known nothing at all. Had my father always been having affairs? Had my mother put up with it while desperately trying to spy on him and running from angry Canadians? For years, perhaps, they had not been the people I thought they were.

"Yes, over, I promise you, sweetheart. Oh, there was that one night a while ago when he came by for coffee and conversations, but that was meaningless. I mean it. Just friendly."

"Sure," I said stupidly.

"I'm glad you believe me. I wanted to be your friend, but it's kind of awkward, you know what I mean?" She clasped my hands again. "So, now we're gonna be friends, right?"

"Sure," I said.

*

I sat on a bench on the boardwalk crying for a long time after that. My parents were no longer just embarrassingly eccentric. They were turning into people I knew nothing about. Strangers I might not even want to meet.

David sat next to me, rocking me back and forth like someone's mother would do. For a while he sang Christmas carols quietly, because even though it was night it was still very hot and humid, and he insisted that Christmas songs would make us feel cooler. Finally, he stopped, and we just sat there in the darkness, listening to the ocean.

My parents were asleep when I got back to the house. I grabbed a family size box of Saltines and some of my mother's cigarettes and locked myself in my room for several days. My mother knocked at the door many times, trying to get me to come out. My father even stood at the door for a while and told me a funny story about a seagull. But I wouldn't come out, except to sneak into the bathroom when the house was quiet.

A couple of nights later I was lying in my room, drinking from a bottle of limoncello that I had stolen from Roderigo and Betty's kitchen when they had us over for dinner earlier in the summer. My father was working. My mother had the night off and had left around 4, saying she was going to dinner with Zell and Sophie, two old friends who were staying in Driftwood for a week. Around 8, there was a loud banging at the door. I ignored it for a while, but the person kept coming back, so I finally got up. It was the guy from next door, a man in his 60s or so named Stu. He had an annoyed look on his face when I opened the door. He was wearing an undershirt and black dress pants and was rubbing his chin, which was covered with silvery stubble.

"You been here the whole time, young lady?"

"Yeah."

"Didn't you hear me knocking?"

"Can I help you?"

He pursed his lips, then sighed and went on.

"You know we have a phone over at our place."

"That's nice."

He stopped again, opened his mouth, thought better of it and shook his head.

"Okay, look, I do your parents a favor, let them give people our number in case they need to get in touch with you in a hurry?"

I nodded. Stu and his wife had come over with messages before.

He was hesitating again. "Well, honey, I got a call from someone in Atlantic City. About your mom? I guess she's not feeling well. She needs someone to come get her." He stopped, sighed again, and looked at me appraisingly. "Is your dad home?"

"No, but why did someone call from Atlantic City?"

"That's where she is. At the Pierpont Hotel. You know it?"

I nodded.

"Well, that's where she is. Guy named Herbie called. You know a guy named Herbie?"

I nodded.

"Well, so, I guess you'll know what to do then?" He was edging backwards from the door now but still eyeing me with some concern. "When will your dad be home?"

"Soon," I blurted. "Any minute." It was actually at least two hours before my father closed the show at Curly's.

"Thankssomuchwe'llbefinenow," I told him, waving idiotically as I edged the door shut. I threw some things into a purse, then lowered myself out my bedroom window into the backyard, so that Stu and his wife, Lindy, wouldn't see me leaving the house alone. The air that night was soupy, humid and overcast. I made my way along the sandy alleyways and through backyards until I got to the end of the street, then I took off and ran the blocks to the Meterrys' house. Now it was me banging on their door, slamming my fist on it over and over.

"Okay, okay, what the hell?" A sleepy looking David stuck his head out. "What?" he said, snapping alert when he saw me.

"I gotta go to Atlantic City."

"OK, I'll drive you there." I followed him through the house, not even noticing that he was pulling off pajamas and changing into jeans and a T-shirt.

"How are we going to get a car?" I asked.

"I know a guy," David said. "Wait here." He bolted out the front door and ran down the road. I sat in the silence, surrounded by seashore souvenirs and family photos. Since their house was a few blocks closer to the beach, I imagined I could hear the waves crashing. After a few minutes, I heard a car wheezing down the road. David drove up in an ancient Opel Caravan, a weird kind of European station wagon.

"Do you have a license?" I asked as we screeched out onto the Garden State Parkway.

"I'm a very good driver," he said.

"Did you steal this car?"

"I told you, I know a guy."

"How come someone who never talks to anyone knows so many guys?"

He just smiled and went back to driving somewhat erratically down the highway. We were going abnormally slowly, with our shaky headlights illuminating a seemingly endless right-hand lane.

It seemed to take us forever to get to Atlantic City. Once off the highway, we drove past streets with boarded-up buildings and then small houses and restaurants until we reached Pacific Avenue, the street that ran parallel to the boardwalk. David finally pulled into a spot near the hotel. It had once been two hotels right across the street from each other, built in the 1860s and modernized with boxy 1960s additions. Indoors that night, it smelled of cigarette smoke and the fishy odor that sometimes wafted up from the beach.

My mother was sitting in the lobby, wearing a long skirt and hair arranged on top of her head. If she had seen herself, she would have said she looked like an animatronic version of Abe Lincoln's wife, waxy and unreal. The dazed expression on her face made her look like some of the ladies you saw on the benches on Broadway sometimes, someone who shouldn't have been let out alone in the world.

She didn't seem particularly surprised or interested to see us. She smiled knowingly and said, "Well, everything's over now, isn't it?"

"Hi, Mrs. Harris," David said, earnest and even. "We've come to give you a ride home."

She looked at him as if he had told her a mildly interesting scientific fact. "Reeeeely," she said.

Herbie shuffled over, appearing from behind one of the lobby's many marble columns. "Hey," he said.

"Where have you been? Why did you leave her alone?" I hissed.

He shrugged. "I... saw somebody I knew."

"Why is she like this?"

He looked around uncomfortably. "I think she came to see Larry. There might have been a misunderstanding."

"Where is Larry?"

Herbie looked at me and snorted. "Gone for good, toots. His gig here ended yesterday and he moved to Vegas. He's got a long-term booking at a new casino there, the Fountains. He's set for life." There was a silence while I took this in. "I couldn't go with him right away," Herbie added. "I… have some commitments here. They love me in Atlantic City. I really pull in the crowds." We looked around the lobby, which was nearly empty.

"You just never know, but it all makes sense in the end, doesn't it?" my mother said, still talking to an invisible audience across the room. I had been sort of assuming she wasn't really too conscious of other people, so I turned quickly to see how she was reacting to my conversation with Herbie. It seemed to have no impact. I looked at David and could tell that we were both wondering whether it was best to continue to treat her gently—like an accident victim—or if it was time to try to snap her out of it and drag her to the car.

"Dorothy Harris?" A fat couple from Philadelphia stood over her. They seemed like nice enough people, but there was no other way to describe them. My mother tilted her head up to them at a weird angle and smiled graciously.

The wife, who had a cap of soft blond curls and short, ring-filled hands, leaned toward her. "We saw you at Geronimo's in the Poconos last year. You were wonderful. The glowworm, it was a hoot. Are you working here?"

My mother shook her head. "No, Curly's Sea Shack, in Driftwood, open six nights a week. No cover, and parking in the rear." She smiled maniacally and waved her arm regally, possibly in the direction of Driftwood.

"Time to go, my dear." David took the opportunity to grab her hand and smoothly yank her up so sharply that she turned to him in a moment of lucid annoyance. Before I followed them out, Herbie touched my arm.

"I'm sorry about your mom, kid," he said. "I know Larry loves her, but like a sister, you know? He's a funny guy. Likes to please people, you know what I mean? Tells them what they want to hear. Makes a lot of promises." He paused for a moment and sighed. "I'm sure you'll hear from him down the road, like nothing happened. 'Hey, how's my best friend,' that kind of thing. He's done that to me a couple of times, to be honest with you. And… some other women. That's just Larry. So, I think there was a misunderstanding. He loves your dad, you know? And I'm sure he's not into, you know, older gals."

We watched David and my mother disappear as they walked down the long set of stairs to the boardwalk.

*

I gave up on locking myself in my room. If I did it again, Stu or Lindy or who knows who else would probably shinny down from the roof and climb through my window to demand I clean up after whatever antics my parents were going to come up with next. I did sleep in the next day, leaving my room at around 2. I strode down to the beach. It was late August by then, and the crowds were growing even thinner as families went home and began to prepare for school. I sat there throughout the afternoon, throwing stones into the water, as angry once again as the night that David and I visited Yolanda. These days, it seemed hard to find anyone to like.

Late in the afternoon, my mother showed up and sat beside me. She still looked waxen and insane, but now she was very interested in talking.

"What is it?" she asked. "You've found out something bad, haven't you? About your dad?"

"About Dad?" I said. "What about you? What about what I've found out about you?"

She shook her head very hard in tiny little shakes and waved her finger close to my nose. "No," she hissed. "That was nothing. Never mind. A misunderstanding. But Yolanda told you something, didn't she? Something bad is going to happen to us, isn't it? The whole world is exploding. I see that now." Her voice was ragged and she was paler than usual.

I thought for a long time about what to say, but I came up empty. "Just get away from me," I told her finally. I got up and began looking for bigger stones to throw in the water. "I don't want to see you again," I said as I paced. "I don't want to be your private detective, your messenger girl, your retirement fund, your psychiatrist. I want you away from me."

"What the heck is wrong with you?" she rasped.

"I had you for a mother, that's what. Normal kids don't have to ask women if they're having an affair with their fathers. Normal kids are protected from these things. They don't have to know this much."

"So I'm not normal. So sue me." She shrugged elaborately. She was wearing a light white sweater over a sleeveless top and a faux Hermes scarf over her curlers.

"You don't even know the zip code for normal. You're crazy. And that's why Dad hates you."

She got up and slapped me, then grabbed my collar and pulled my face close to hers.

"Listen to me. The two of you are too stupid to know it, but you'd be nothing without me. I watch out for all of our interests. But not anymore. I'm going to go in there tonight, finish my show—because I'm a professional and that's what we do—and then just drop dead. Because you've worn me out, the two of you. The whole damn world. So I'll just drop dead and then you'll be happy."

She pushed me away so hard that I fell backwards onto the beach. Then she strode up the sand toward the boardwalk, the wind whipping at her scarf and her clothes as she went.

128

Curly's was packed that night, despite the fact that the town was emptying out. David and I sat in a booth near the door, eating french fries and doing a crossword puzzle. People clapped along when the Meterry Sisters sang "Stop in the Name of Love," and they gave Reynolds and Yolanda a standing ovation.

My mother was next. Yolanda, leaving the stage, tripped and fell to her knees as my mother zigzagged a little as she pushed the xylophone past her. My mother gave her a big apologetic smile and Yolanda smiled back through gritted teeth. My mother came to center stage and began playing her opening song, "Flight of the Bumblebee," a fast, lively number. She was fully in control and doing well. When she was finished, the audience clapped enthusiastically and she raised her arms in triumph.

She smiled, her face at first delighted. Then the life in her eyes was suddenly gone and her features went slack. She slumped face first over the xylophone.

The crowd gasped. Curly, who was the bandleader that night, jumped down from the bandstand and rushed over to her. He lifted her into his arms and took her pulse, first on her wrist, then on her neck. He shook her a little and seemed to be speaking to her. He looked up slowly at the audience.

"Oh no," he said.

There was a sound then, a low moaning sound like an animal in pain. I tried to see where it was coming from, but everyone in the room seemed to be looking in my direction. And then suddenly David was yanking me sideways out of the booth.

"Let me through," he shouted as he pulled me backwards through the crowd. "I want to get her out of here."

"No, I have to stay," I tried to shout back, but he kept going until we were in the parking lot.

"I have to go back in," I yelled. "You think she's dead or something, but I know she's not. I have to go back in. I have to go in there. I have to help her."

"I know, I know," he kept repeating in a quiet voice. "We'll see her in a minute." He was behind me so I kicked backwards at whatever I could reach, jammed my elbows into his ribs and tried poking his eyes out with my thumbs, but he just held on to me, his arms firmly around my ribs.

Chapter 15

Imagine an idyllic setting. A stone archway opens onto lush manicured lawns. The words "Oak Shade Cemetery" are carved into the stone. An elegant hearse drives through the gateway and turns to the right, followed by a long line of black limousines and expensive dark cars.

Once they have passed, an ancient hearse pulls up to the gateway, moving very slowly—laboring, you might say—leading a long line of dusty, decrepit convertibles, sagging Volkswagen vans and flashy but not terribly new sports cars. They turn left as they move through the gate. The last car carries a sign that says "Goodbye, Dorothy" and has black crepe paper streaming from the bumper. That second one was my mother's funeral procession.

A lot of people came. Banjo players, jugglers, accordionists, hypnotists. People we would become best friends with for a while when my parents were booked with them out of town, then not see again for months or years. At the end of the service my father and I stood with the Meterry Sisters and David, watching the cemetery workers fill the grave.

"She wasn't so bad, even though she was a class-A bitch," Jenny, the middle Meterry sister, sniffled. Joni shoved her hard in the ribs.

"Come sit over here and talk to me. Please?" David asked. We sat on a marble bench under a tree. The bench was cold, holding on to the early morning chill, and the first falling leaves skittered across the grass.

"How are you doing?" he asked. I hadn't really seen him since the day my mother died. I had been spending a lot of time in my room.

"Okay."

"Ginger, I'm going to be going to college soon. In Boston. In five days."

"Great."

"I was thinking…. I was thinking you could come with me. We can—I can afford to get a little apartment. I could sleep on the couch, you know. You can finish high school there. When you're done with telephone lineman school—or whatever—we'll go away. We'll do all the things we said we would. Dance on the Pont Neuf. You know?"

"What, and leave show business?"

David smiled hopefully, but the joke had come out despite myself. Ever since my mother died, I had felt as if I was watching life on TV, as if all the people around me were putting on a show. People ask how you feel. Did you miss her something awful? Were you holding back the tears? Was your stomach churning? Were you having nightmares? Did you want to howl in pain? But that wasn't how I felt at all. Mostly, I felt as if there was some dreary TV show spinning along in front of me. That was how David seemed to me now. Like someone on TV, advertising something that had nothing to do with me.

I shook my head when he was finished talking and shrugged. "I don't think so."

"But, you know, Paris?" he said.

Paris. An apartment in Boston. I could hitch my wagon to his success and have them both, maybe. So far, though, being part of an entourage did not seem to be working out so well for me. I envisioned myself carrying David's sheet music cases from concert hall to concert hall.

And lately I had been thinking a lot about something that had happened in school right before the end of the last term. I had this

English teacher named Ms. Mannocchi. Although my typical reaction to teachers—really almost anyone—was pity, this woman appeared to be funny and smart, and she treated us as if we were adults, which caught my attention. She was a short woman with a thick head of short hair. She was probably only in her 20s, but she had a serious air that made you think she would become some beloved college professor or a Supreme Court justice, or something. So, anyway, she came up to me during exam time. We hadn't talked much during the year, because I generally didn't talk much. But she had given me good grades and seemed to get my sense of humor. So, she stopped me and said, "I've realized something about you." I smiled blandly, my usual first line of defense. "You're a hell of a lot smarter than you pretend to be." Now she had my attention, although I was skeptical of her intentions.

"I'm putting together a list for next year's AP English class," she continued. "I want to recommend you, but are you up for the work? It's a very demanding class."

Can anyone resist a request—a challenge, really—from someone who claims we have promise? All of a sudden, despite all my better instincts, I had felt a surge of excitement about the adventures I could have if I was the smart, competent girl I thought I had glimpsed in Ms. Mannocchi's eyes. Even though I always tried to be the level-headed one who kept her head down, it was an idea I had been toying with all summer long as I thought of the next school year: Be the smart girl and see what happens.

And now I wondered what direction this circus would lurch off into, would I end up having to follow my father or David? Maybe my best idea was to count on myself. That was something I'd always done, of course, but maybe this was my first chance to really commit to the idea.

Looking at David now, I said, "I don't know what you're talking about. Those are nice ideas, but I don't want to be a starving artist. I told you that. I don't want to be the last in a long line of unhappy endings."

He pushed a strand of hair out of my face and smiled. It was a gentle and lovely smile. "Don't worry, Ginger," he said. "I'll take care of you."

"You'll take care of me?" All of a sudden I was angry. I looked at him, my eyes not quite focused. "Take care of me? That's what you think I want? That's what you think is good for me? Nobody has ever taken care of me. I don't need that. You think you're going to come in on a white horse and take me away?" I was shouting now. "Well, listen, buddy, I can get my own stupid horse. I can rescue myself. Do you understand? Do you have any idea what I'm saying?"

He was pale and wide-eyed. "Yes, I think you've made yourself clear," he said finally.

He kept trying, though. He followed me around the cemetery for a while, kind and respectful, but with enough of his old quiet, menacing self that he didn't annoy me too much. And of course our families were thrown together now. Usually, in a case like this, the two adulterers would wait a decent time to reunite and start a new life together. But everything had been blown up at the end of that summer, it turned out, not just my mother's life and our family, but also the kind of show business life my father would lead. So we skipped the formalities and Julie and my father became a couple immediately, which means we weren't going to get away from the Meterrys. David and I silently negotiated a truce, going back to something like the way we were before we thought we might be in love. One day, before he left for school, I took him to Funland in Times Square and taught him to play skee ball. Then he took me to a jazz club in a basement off 8th Avenue in the 40s. There was an obese woman playing piano and singing like Bessie Smith, and a waiter whose eyes each went in a different direction. I really could imagine my father—his observant, bemused self—loving a place like this, taking in the weirdness of it. And I could certainly imagine my mother hating it, not charmed by the raffish shabbiness or the crowd, which seemed to be made up of adoring young people in black and elderly men in fedoras. "Nobodies on a night out," I could imagine her

134

saying. But the place was packed, with people overjoyed not just at being there, but at having found a place in the world together that was so much damn fun. 'This is what life will be like if you go to Boston with him,' I thought, and I almost changed my mind and packed a bag. But I didn't.

I know. You're thinking, give the guy a chance, right? But I was determined not to hop right on to someone else's road show right then. I wanted to be just me, fresh off the Tsunami, shaky but still alive. And needing to find my own solid ground.

Epilogue

After that, everyone went their separate ways. Reynolds and Yolanda bought Curly's, turned it into a disco called the Inferno and made a fortune. My father and Julie put together a song and dance act, calling themselves the RazzleDazzles, and began performing on cruise ships. They got married about six months after my mother died, in a ceremony at the Municipal Building in Manhattan. They looked so happy that I hated them for a while.

They were away a lot of the time, so they sent me to live with Julie's sisters, Joni and Jenny. The sisters had bought a little house in a small town in New Jersey because they wanted to be close to New York, where they planned to make it big in show business. I have to admit that they were tremendously patient and kind to me, even though I hardly spoke to them for the first year I lived with them. On weekend nights, they would give me facials and braid my hair into a French braid, always trying to start conversations about classes and boys and my dreams for the future. Then I would put on my black makeup again and iron my hair flat. They insisted that becoming a telephone lineman was a great idea and wanted to know all about what I thought I would wear when I became one and what kinds of adventures I would have when I fixed the phones of celebrities.

David went to college. On most of his holidays he traveled to a performance or workshop somewhere, so we saw him very rarely.

I finished high school while I was living with Joni and Jenny, at a big regional school in New Jersey, one that was full of tanned, hardy farm kids or people who played tennis. I doggedly kept to my plan of being the smart girl that Ms. Mannocchi had seen, and that became my hope for the future. There was no one like Ms. Mannocchi there, but I decided she had given me enough momentum that I might be able to keep going on my own.

It was a funny place to live. In New York, you had to find the silence and wrap yourself in it for a while so you could be alone. In that farm town, the silence surrounded you. At lunch at school, I had a table to myself in the cafeteria. For a while the junior varsity football team would throw food at me, but I think the guidance counselor made them stop.

It was all right, though, because along the way I had decided that my mother had actually been right. So I knew I just had to bide my time.

Here is what I told myself: I am the worm. And if I can just find the right light, I will truly glow.

The End

Anita Dennis is an award-winning writer whose work has appeared in the *New York Times* and the *Wall Street Journal*, among other publications.